RIPTIDES

CAROL MOREIRA

Cover design: Rebekah Wetmore
Editor: Andrew Wetmore

ISBN: 978-1-990187-20-9
First edition November, 2021

2475 Perotte Road
Annapolis County, NS
B0S 1A0

moosehousepress.com
info@moosehousepress.com

We live and work in Mi'kma'ki, the ancestral and unceded territory of the Mi'kmaw people. This territory is covered by the "Treaties of Peace and Friendship" which Mi'kmaw and Wolastoqiyik (Maliseet) people first signed with the British Crown in 1725. The treaties did not deal with surrender of lands and resources but in fact recognized Mi'kmaq and Wolastoqiyik (Maliseet) title and established the rules for what was to be an ongoing relationship between nations. We are all Treaty people.

For Peter, my own Nova Scotian

This is a work of fiction. The author has created the characters, conversations, interactions, and events; and any resemblance of any character to any real person is coincidental.

Contents

Carol Moreira

1: It's illegal

Cam grimaces and breathes through the pain. *It's good for you*, he tells himself as he levers the olive-green pile of rockweed out of the water and into his boat. *That burning means you're building muscle. One day, you might even make the football team.*

But his pulse jumps with alarm as his boat rocks beneath his feet. He's moved too fast and nearly tipped *Ashley*.

He pauses a moment, then begins to ease the fronds of slimy seaweed from his rake. He's gotta be careful—the pile of rockweed in the centre of his boat is growing. If he tips *Ashley*, he'll lose the valuable harvest.

The new rockweed slithers onto the weed already piled in the boat. The dense, salty scent of the air bladders and the sight of them swollen with oxygen remind Cam of finding rockweed with his father. As a kid, he'd loved popping the air bladders. They seemed round as balloons, fat and fun, like the air bubbles in packaging.

But those days are gone. His dad has deserted him

and disappeared off to Toronto. The only thing that matters now is making money.

Cam stares at the glistening pile of rockweed. How much will he get for it? A couple of hundred? He's got another $100 from restaurant tips. He needs to harvest more dulse and sand dollars. Tourists love the red seaweed and pretty shells, and they're easier work than dragging rockweed from the ocean.

He wonders if he can squeeze one more load into the boat. Deciding to go for it, he leans out, dropping the rake into the slimy seaweed that floats like thick, knotted hair on the water's surface.

It feels like the plants are sticking together, as if they don't want him disturbing them. But he must, and he raises the rake and sinks its teeth down into the middle of the rockweed. He hauls it out, being careful not to wrench the plants from their roots or sever them too low—if he takes too much, there'll be no rockweed in the future.

As he pulls the weed from the rake, he thinks how sinewy and strong it feels. *Everything has its own life. Everything wants to survive.*

"Okay, Mick," he says, turning to his dog, who is lying, bored, in the boat's bow. "Time to go."

Mick turns and barks, short and sharp, as if to stress that Cam has taken too long.

Cam grins. "Okay, old boy. I know you don't like the water."

Switching on the engine, he nods as the motor chugs to life. He swings *Ashley* for shore and soon reaches the sandy edge of the beach. This load will be valuable. It's a shame disease has killed the sea urchins that restaurants want for sushi, but this is good.

As he drags *Ashley* up the sand, Mick barks, a brisk warning. Cam glances at his dog and sees him standing erect, his black ears alert, staring into the trees where Stony River empties into the ocean.

Cam gazes into the leafy shade and sees John emerging through the branches. "Hi!" Cam is glad to see his life-long friend.

"Woof!" Mick rushes at John, expecting to be patted.

But John ignores Mick. "Stay away from me, dumb ass." He glares at Cam. "Your dad's an idiot. My dad says so."

"What's happened?" Cam's gut heaves. Their dads have been arguing about jobs since the fish stocks fell and the work dried up.

"Ask your old man. Your dad thought he deserved last place on Jack's boat. He even took a swing at my dad. And my dad's been fishing with Jack for ages."

Alarm flickers over Cam's skin. John has been away at cadet camp. It's been weeks since they saw each other, and in that time John's grown. He's always been big, but now his neck and jaw, his chest and arms, are thick and threatening.

John stares at *Ashley*, at the mound of glistening rockweed in the motorboat's centre. "You don't have a permit to harvest that."

"I do," Cam lies. He feels his face flush.

"Yeah, right. You're too young. It's illegal."

"I told you, I've got one. I'm using a friend's."

John snickers. "You're a crap liar, O'Connell. And you're weird—just like your dad. Your granddad, too."

"Shut up!" Rage pulses through Cam. His grandfather's only recently died. His grandfather was always kind to John.

John's eyes move over Cam's body. "Why are you so short, midget?" He strides forward and shoves Cam's chest. Cam staggers, almost tumbling back into *Ashley* and the load of rockweed.

"Midget," John says. Then he turns and stalks away. In a minute he has disappeared among the trees.

Cam stares at the spot where John had stood. He feels sick.

"Woof!" Mick leans into Cam and licks his knees. He brushes his tail against Cam's legs.

"What the heck was that about, Mick?" Cam bends to stroke his pet. "John ignored you, boy, didn't he?"

Cam ruffles Mick's fur behind the ears, but he feels like he's swallowed one of Wreck Island's big, grey rocks. Their dads had a flight—that's why John didn't reply to his texts. Cam had assumed the phone coverage was poor at John's camp. But he should have known there was a problem.

Everything's about money now—the lack of it. The fight must have happened before his dad left for Toronto. That was six weeks ago. John's been angry all this time. He's been hanging on to his anger the whole time he was at camp.

Cam pulls out his phone, dials a number and speaks softly. "Kevin," he says. "I've got a load, a good one....Yeah, see you on the beach."

He tucks the phone inside his pocket and stares at the rockweed. He should be glad because of the money. But he's furious—with John, and with his dad who's disappeared off to Toronto and left Cam and his mum with nothing but sadness and bills.

He strides about the sand, tries to calm down, but his anger feels like a volcano bursting out of his belly. It's pulsing through him, hot and energetic.

He stops and stares at the calm blue water and the distant outlines of tiny islands. His shoulders slump as the peace begins to seep into him. The splash and ripple of the waves is soothing, but it summons his sadness.

He misses his dad. His father is always at the back of his mind. His dad used to talk about seeing the ghost of a dead pirate on Wreck Island, and now it feels almost like his father is the ghost. *Dad's haunting me. It's creepy.*

"Hey, Cam!"

Cam looks over his shoulder and sees Kevin ambling down the beach.

"Great load," Kevin says as he approaches and sees the rockweed.

"Thanks." Cam forces a grin. "Let's offload it." John's right about the permit.

"Don't worry, Mr. Nervous," Kevin says with a patronizing grin.

Cam flushes. Kevin is old, at least 40. He needn't act like Cam's a kid. *Calm down. The tourists, the food and beauty companies all want seaweed. You'll soon have enough money to help Mom keep the house.*

He grins a better grin this time. Kevin thinks Cam is 16, when he's only 13. He's tricked Kevin. *I'm small but I'm strong. We can shift this lot quick, and then I'll go home and eat.*

2: Buried treasure

Cam tells his mom about his encounter with John.

"No...really?" She frowns and puts her cup back on the table. "That's bullying. John's older than you; he's already 14. Ignore him," she says and a furrow grows in her forehead. "Whatever's happened between your dads, you two shouldn't get involved. Anyway, your dad's in Toronto now. Let it be."

Cam frowns, too. "Who knows if I'll ever talk to Dad again..."

"Cam, you know your dad gives you all the time he can."

His mom looks away, over to the windowsill where there's a photo of Cam's father hauling in a net that's heavy and silvery with halibut. His dad is smiling at the camera, his eyes blue. His arms and hands look strong and sinewy as they hold the full net. Cam's mom sighs and her eyes travel to the trees bending in the breeze outside."You know money's all the fishermen think about these days."

Cam nods. "Yup."

His mom leans across the table and rubs his arm. "Don't be sad, Cam. This will pass. Now, eat up."

She picks up her fork. "The realtor's bringing someone to see the house at six. We need to eat fast."

Cam picks up the jug of maple syrup and pours a golden pool over his stack of French toast, but his appetite has gone. "Who's coming?"

His mom shrugs. "Just someone who's interested in buying our house. More people are moving out of town since the pandemic. It'll be easier to sell."

Cam cuts his toast and puts a piece in his mouth. He tries to focus on the delicious taste of maple syrup, cinnamon and egg, but he feels sick at the thought of strangers living in his home. He can't imagine still being himself if he has to live somewhere else. What if he has to move to Halifax? The country is the only place where you can feel comfortable and get away from people.

"How much do we need so we can stay?" he says when he's swallowed two mouthfuls of toast and a piece of sausage.

"Cam. Forget it, love. We can't do it. I don't earn much at the pre-school and your dad has new expenses now."

Cam sighs. "How. Much. Do. We. Need. To. Stay?"

"It doesn't matter, Cam."

Anger heats him. "Don't treat me like a kid."

His mom's eyes tear up and Cam feels guilty. His eyes fall from hers to Mick, who's waiting hopefully beneath the table.

"Okay then," his mom says. "It's $50,000."

Cam swallows. She's right—it's too much. He feels like a fool. His rockweed and dulse money, the sand dollars, the cash he gets for clearing tables at the restaurant, even added up they don't come close. His efforts seem...pathetic.

"We should sell soon, while the weather's good," his mom says. "We're beside the ocean. People pay more for ocean views and access."

Anger flashes through Cam. People are mean, hoping to profit from his family's troubles. And all these city people coming in. They're driving up house prices. Communities won't be the same when they're full of city folks working on laptops. The restaurants, the cafes—they're already changing, getting city smart, expensive.

"We might have to move closer to Halifax," his mom says. "Or maybe we could find a little place in Bedford..."

"Mom, I'm not moving there," Cam interrupts. His mom doesn't even realize that Bedford is part of Halifax. Bedford is nothing but streets and cars.

"I still can't believe Dad's walked out on us," he says.

His mom's eyes grow even shinier. "Cam, your dad loves *you*."

Cam snickers. "Yeah, right." He glances at the picture of his father holding the fishing net. "All we've got left of Dad is photos. It's like he's that dead pirate."

His mom smiles. "Don't believe that silly ghost story, Cam. All that nonsense about Sir Stamford burying stolen treasure on Wreck Island. Your dad and granddad got so excited when your granddad found Sir Stamford's diary. It was...daft." She frowns. "People don't find treasure or win the lottery, Cam. People like us work hard for our money."

Cam says nothing. He doesn't like hearing his dad and granddad criticized, but they did get kinda crazy over the rumours of buried treasure. His dad's obsession grew worse as the fishing got bad. He even bought a metal detector on Kijiji and dragged it all over Wreck Island. He found nothing but ancient Coke cans and bits of shoe and belt buckle. After that, his dad started playing the Lottery. Cam's mom didn't like that.

Cam looks at his mother's sweet face and wonders what went wrong between his parents. His mom is funny and kind, hard-working and good-looking. It's not her fault the fish stocks declined. The stocks were over-fished, and that's the government's fault and the scientists' fault. Cam feels like punching his dad for being cruel to his mom.

"And don't offer me your money," his mom says. "That's your cash. Don't worry, Cam. I'll find a house that's nice, and big enough for us two."

Cam nods. He doesn't tell his mom he's harvesting rockweed without a permit. Maybe he shouldn't be taking the risk, but he can't stop. They need money. And he must do something.

He looks at his plate and slips a chunk of sausage under the table for Mick.

"Cam!" his mom says as Mick's jaws snap. "Don't feed Mick at mealtimes."

Cam scowls and pushes his plate away. "I'm not hungry. I'm going to my room."

"Okay. Don't let John bother you, love."

Cam takes his plate to the sink. As he goes down to his basement bedroom, he decides to listen to some fiddling by Ashley MacIsaac. He's loved the fiddle ever since he first heard traditional Scottish music at school. The music made him feel so many emotions. The sounds the fiddle makes—eerily beautiful yet harsh—spoke to him, although he wasn't sure what they were saying.

Cam had known he was hearing the music of his Scottish ancestors, but he'd never felt the connection before. Now, that music feels personal. He has a better understanding of its moods and tones. And MacIsaac is the best. His tunes are wild and free; they make Cam's feet and spirit jump.

He smiles. *The Devil in the Kitchen:* that's the sound he needs.

Carol Moreira

3: Your family must be ghosts

"Dev, let's go."

Dev keeps kicking the dead tree.

"Dev, come *on*." Anika tries to sound mean, like the woman who was her first-grade teacher in England.

Dev shakes his head. "Leave me alone or I'll tell Dad you brought me here."

Anika sighs and crawls inside the little tent she had constructed out of her old pink dress and some twigs. Canada is so hot. But the air is stifling in her shelter and she wriggles out and plonks herself down on a big grey rock. Usually, Anika can get her kid brother to do what she wants, but sometimes Dev gets as hard to move as the rock she's sitting on.

She watches Dev and feels a heaviness in her chest. It's loneliness. She first learned to identify the feeling during lockdown in London. If only she knew some kids her own age in Nova Scotia.

She's desperate to find new friends, but she's scared. The CBC had a story about a Black kid who'd been sitting on a beach, and some white kids came over and waved a noose in his face.

Anika had felt her entire body shrink and tremble as longing for her friends in London filled her. Now, she blinks hard – she will not cry in front of Dev.

Dev's tree has tipped over and pulled its skinny white roots from the ground. Her brother's foot is making chips of mud and root fly. He bends down and picks up long pieces of root, which he tucks away in a pocket of his red shorts.

"You're weird, Dev," Anika says. "Why do you stuff junk in your pockets?"

"This tree looks like a burned-up space ship. The roots are electric wires." And he starts kicking again.

Kick, kick. It's the only sound Anika hears. Her eyes close, but she jumps awake when a loud rattling starts up nearby.

She spins around but sees only a red squirrel bolting up a branch. The squirrel stops and his tail begins bouncing off his back in time to the rattling. He looks like he's doing a weird dance.

Another sound—twigs cracking. Anika's heart leaps. Is it a bear? There are black bears in Nova Scotia. If they see one, they must retreat slowly with lowered eyes.

But it's not a bear. It's a guy. He's pale-skinned but tanned, with curly dark hair. He's wearing worn denim shorts and a white T-shirt that's grown too small. The stretched fabric reveals the muscles that are beginning to bulge in his chest and arms. He carries a fishing rod. A little dog with black fur stands beside him.

"Hi," he says with a grin.

Anika doesn't reply. She looks at her brother. Dev is watching the intruder, his eyes big and round beneath his red maple-leaf sunhat.

"Why are you on our island?" Dev says. Anika is glad Dev says that, although of course it's not their island.

The guy frowns. "It's not *your* island."

Anika studies him. She figures he's about 13, like her. He speaks in a slow, drawling way. Nova Scotians speak like they have all the time in the world. It's annoying. She doesn't have all day to listen to them drag their sentences out.

Her eyes linger on this guy's sinewy arms and she feels her face flush. She looks away and smooths her new shorts over her thighs. She's glad she's wearing the yellow ones. The colour suits her.

"We were here first," Dev says.

The stranger shakes his head. "I've been here lots of times and I've never seen you, little guy."

Dev's face flushes, he squirms. "We made a tent." He points to the shelter Anika made from her old dress.

The guy smirks as he looks at the pink cloth flapping in the breeze. "That'll be useless in the wind."

Anika feels her own flush deepen. She stares at the stranger as he stares at her. His eyes are a bright blue. The suntan around them makes them look bluer, like the sea or sky.

"What kind of tent would *you* make?" Dev says.

The guy shrugs. "Don't need to. I have my motorboat and a kayak. I have an ATV too, although I prefer boats."

"You have boats and an ATV?" Dev's eyes grow huge. "ATVs are like cars, but better."

"I can't stand ATVs," Anika says. "They're noisy and dirty and they rip up the countryside."

"Not necessarily," the stranger says and a frown crosses his face. "They're fun to ride in the woods. You can go for miles."

Anika shakes her head. "ATVs are just like all the other vehicles killing the planet."

The stranger frowns deeper but says nothing.

"I'd love to go in a boat," Dev says. He looks down at the little dog, which is circling his legs and wagging its tail, desperate for attention. "I don't like that we have to walk to this island over the sand. It's boring. We should get to swim or go in a boat."

"Maybe I'll take you out," the stranger says. "I'm Cameron—Cam."

"I'm Dev, and she's my sister, Anika," Dev says. What's your dog called?"

"Mick."

Dev crouches and pets Mick, who flaps his tail hard against Dev's legs. "We moved here last week, from London," he says.

"I've never been to Ontario," Cam says.

"London's in England," Anika tells him.

"Oh, *that* London," Cam says. "There's also a London in Ontario."

Anika flushes deeper.

"My family came from Scotland," Cam tells Dev,

"Hundreds of years ago. And my mom's French—from New Brunswick."

"*Hundreds* of years?" Dev jumps up. "Oooooooh! Your family must be ghosts." And his voice goes high and wobbly as he waves his arms around in a silly impression of a ghost.

Cam chuckles. "Well, I guess they are...Take care, little guy."

And he turns, and he and the dog walk away through the trees.

"Come on, Anika," Dev says. "Let's get to the top of the island and see where he goes."

Dev runs and Anika follows. From the island's summit, they watch Cameron walk across the sandbar and turn left along the beach toward another little island. Like Anika and Dev's island, that island is a tiny circle covered in Christmas trees. Anika sees many other small islands out in the bay. She hadn't realized there were so many islands in Nova Scotia.

She watches Cam become a tiny dot in the distance and feels sad. Maybe he could have been her friend. There must be people in Nova Scotia who aren't racist. But she isn't sure about Cam. He talks so slowly. That could be because he's Nova Scotian, or it could mean he's not very smart. And, despite all his talk about boats and ATVs, Cam's clothes are shabby. He's not like her. His parents are probably not scientists, like hers.

Dev turns to Anika. "This place is an adventure."

Anika reaches out and hugs her brother. He's only eight and annoying, but sometimes she feels how much she loves him. The feeling comes over her in the same way the tide washes over rocks.

Dev lets her hug him then wriggles free and glances over his shoulder. "I need to pee."

"Go in there." Anika points into the darkness among the trees. She watches Dev disappear among the tall trunks and smiles. She's discovered she loves peeing outside. It feels daring and free. The air feels cool on your skin, and your pee steams when it hits damp earth.

Alone, she gazes at the wild, green island, then turns to the bright sea gleaming in the bay. Beyond the bay, the ocean stretches, too vast and deep to imagine. She can hear the surge of waves. The big ones make a distant roar—very different to the gentler, splashing of nearer waves as they curl over the island's shore.

This place is beautiful and clean...hopeful. She inhales the island's salty and sweet summer scents, then dances, flinging her arms to the sky.

As Dev re-appears, she spins to a stop and watches him walk toward her, her pulse still dancing. *I never knew how wonderful the world is until I came here.*

She pulls out her cell phone to capture the sun polishing the water. She'll put the photos online. She's hoping her London friends will see them and decide to come visit.

Loneliness fills her again as she thinks of her friends. At night, when she's in bed in the big, new house, Anika misses knowing that her friends are sleeping in their own homes nearby. She longs for the close, friendly walls and bright, city colours of London.

Loneliness. It's a problem.

4: Rise on a wave

Cam sighs. Now he has another problem. How can he keep on harvesting rockweed with that Anika and her kid brother hanging out on Wreck Island? They're bound to see him. They could go gossiping to their parents or neighbours. And he has no permit.

He frowns, but feels his body heat as he thinks about Anika. He's never seen skin as brown and pretty as hers. Her dark hair curled and waved about her shoulders like it didn't know where to go and her eyes were warm and bright. Looking at Anika had been like staring into the sun.

He sighs again. He can't quit harvesting rockweed. He needs the money. Right now, the tide is out, which means he can harvest dulse along the shoreline. The red-purple seaweed is popular as a health food. The taste isn't great but it's all right if you eat it with something else. Cam's tried dulse instead of bacon in a sandwich and it was okay.

He walks to the store to get some milk for his mom, passing through quiet little Bedford Lane. The houses here are smaller, without the dramatic ocean views his own home provides, but the street feels familiar and peaceful and that soothes his agitation.

He pauses by the monument to the area's fishermen lost at sea. The artistry and beauty of the monument—it shows fishermen heading out on their boat while a woman and child watch from the shore—soothes him, like water does. He understands these images, this emotion. He has stood with his mother on the dock, watching his father power away, and felt that mingled pride and apprehension a fishing family always feels.

He breathes quieter and begins to feel bad about interrupting his mother when she was talking about moving to Bedford. His mom can't help that they have to move. It's his dad who's gone off to Toronto.

In the store, he says 'hi' to Sean, the storekeeper, and then to Kayla, a friend of his mom's he meets heading up the street. *I don't want to move to the city. I know it here, and people know me. This is my community.*

And he feels another surge of hot, sad anger at the thought of the move.

Back home, he delivers the milk to the fridge then heads to the beach with Mick. As he walks, he thinks about his dad's trout story. Before his dad left for Toronto, he told Cam he'd seen an amazing trout swim up Stony River. The fish was the biggest and most beautiful sea trout his dad ever saw.

"His scales were all the colours of the rainbow," his father said, stretching his arms wide. "He was as long as my arm, longer."

Cam wonders if his dad was exaggerating. Probably. But it would be cool to see that trout and cooler to catch it. Maybe he'll stop by Stony River, if there's time.

He reaches the beach and sees his boat bobbing in the water on the far side of Wreck Island. He's left *Ashley* there in case he has time to relax and motor out into the bay. No time for that now though.

He can see dulse scattered across the rocks and shoreline in purply splashes. His feet quicken. Even if he can't save the house, this money will be useful.

He reaches the beach and sloshes through cool water until he reaches the place where the dulse grows thickest. He smiles as he rests his baskets on a rock. The plants look like red lettuce. They look like money.

He reaches into his pocket, takes out his scissors and grips the stem of a dulse plant. It feels strong and sinewy in his hand. Like the rockweed, it resists him.

He cuts; making sure not to take too much. Dulse is like rockweed: you mustn't damage the plant if you want more. *Plants are like fish. If you're greedy they don't replenish.*

He works hard and soon his two baskets are almost full. He grins, thinking how Rosemary at the Seabird Gift Shop will be glad of this lot. The dulse just needs drying and labelling 'health food'. The tourists and the city types will snap it up.

Rosemary will have to dry it herself though. He needs to get back to the rockweed. It's worth more.

The wind strengthens. Cam feels his hair lift in the breeze and sees *Ashley* rise on a wave. He nods at his boat, feeling like a friend has waved to him.

His dad sent him a text saying they might have to sell *Ashley*. The news made Cam's belly churn. *Ashley* is not just a boat, not just a thing. She is Cam's lifelong friend. *Ashley*'s smooth curved lines are as familiar and precious to him as his mother's face.

And *Ashley* takes him out on the ocean. They've had a ton of adventures together. Many times, dolphins and minke whales have swum beside them. The black loops of minkes' backs lifted above the waves as they kept pace with the boat. Once, Cam even saw a humpback leap. The marine giant broke the water and surged into the air. Cam whooped with joy and his skin tingled at the sight.

"Hi! Hi!" Cam found himself yelling at the whale as if he wanted to catch his attention and make friends. The whale was so mysterious, unknown, and yet Cam had felt a kinship; a deep emotion he couldn't name.

Now, in just a few years, he'll be out on the water full-time. Cam's promised his mom he'll graduate high school, but after that he intends to find work on a fishing boat. The lobster and halibut stocks are still good, and the other fish will come back eventually. *I'm going to stay near the ocean. Even if we have to move to the city, I'm never going out west for work like so many people do.*

He harvests the last of the dulse and slowly straightens up, stretching his neck, back and arms.

Then he hoists the baskets and begins to walk toward home, Mick trotting ahead as usual.

He wonders how much the dulse is worth. Maybe he should offer his dad the money. If it's enough, he might be able to keep *Ashley* and the ATV.

When he reaches the spot where the sand becomes wild beach grass, he turns to say goodbye to his boat. He can never leave *Ashley* without a proper farewell.

"See you soon, *Ashley,*" he tells her. "I'll be back real soon."

Carol Moreira

5: Fossils, if you must know

It's astonishing and kind of frightening. The sea mist is so dense and white Anika and Dev can barely see Wreck Island, although they know it has to be nearby.

"It's scary." Dev walks closer to Anika, almost bumping into her legs. "Why's the mist so thick?"

"I don't know." Anika turns and surveys the cloud that covers the ocean. "Maybe the water's a lot colder than the land. That can make fog."

"I wish it would stop," Dev says in a soft, scared voice. "It's like a horror movie, like there's something hiding in the mist. Something that's going to get us."

"When have you ever seen a horror movie?" Anika smiles down at Dev's enormous, fright-filled eyes. Dev never misses a chance to be dramatic.

"I just don't like it."

They walk on and Dev walks even closer, so close he almost trips Anika.

"Dev, watch it!"

He steps back and spins around to point at the sand. "Anika! Look! I can't see our footprints anymore. They've disappeared already. We might get lost in the mist and never find our way out. We could walk into the ocean and be swept away...drowned."

Anika turns and looks. Dev is right. Usually their footprints trail them all the way across the beach, but she can see only the last few imprints left by their bare feet. The indents of their heels, the balls of their feet and the spans of toes remind Anika of when she saw a show about fossilized footprints left by an ancient species of human. Anika had stared at the prints, amazed to think that pre-humans many thousands of years ago had left them. The marks looked so ordinary—she or her friends could have left them.

"Don't worry, Dev," she says now. "We'll just sit here on the beach and wait for the sun to dissolve the mist."

They sit on the damp sand, and it's beautiful to watch the world grow brighter. As the sun becomes higher and hotter, the mist thins and fades until only a few fine wisps cling to the beach and nearby islands.

Dev nods and sighs long and deep with relief. "It's properly day now," he says, unclasping his hands from around his knees. He crouches, getting ready to get up. "But now I miss the mist."

Anika chuckles as she gets to her feet. "Honestly, Dev! Come on. Let's go to the island. It's getting hot already."

It is. Not long after they reach the island, the air is hanging heavy with heat.

"Now I'm melting like ice cream," Dev says. "I'm going in the tent. I'm…"

"What?" Anika says. Dev is staring open-mouthed at a large, grey rock.

"Gold." Dev points.

"Don't be stupid," Anika says, but she sees many golden flecks gleaming inside the rock. The sight makes Anika's heart speed up like it does when she's running as fast as she can in a 100-metre race. That speed, that exertion, is the best feeling in the world, like being lit up and powerful, electrified through your whole body and mind.

"Then what is it?" Dev says.

Anika stares at the rock. Have they stumbled upon their very own stash of gold? No, can't be. Local people wouldn't leave gold lying around. Nova Scotians don't seem very smart, but they wouldn't do that.

"It can't be gold, Dev. It must be something else."

"Well, I'm going to collect some, just in case. You could be wrong. Help me?"

Anika bends and touches the boulder's gleaming centre. The gold stuff feels rough under her skin and a flake rubs off on her finger. She scratches the rock and her nail fills with gold, and glitters and shines. Dev scratches the gold too and chuckles when his nail turns yellow.

"Amazing," Anika says.

"It's in the *ground* there!" Dev shouts and points. Golden chunks as big as chocolate chips lie in the sandy earth. "It's gold! Gold!"

"Shush." Anika kneels and picks the chips from the earth. Dev does the same and they hold the soft, flaky gold in their hands.

"Here." Anika puts her gold down for a moment and opens up her backpack. "Put it in here, Dev. Don't shove it in your pockets."

They're so busy separating the gold from the earth and sand, they don't hear the dog bark, and they jump to their feet as a little dog with black fur rushes from the trees. It's Mick, he belongs to that guy—Cam.

Anika swings the backpack over her shoulder as Cam appears from among the branches.

"Hi," he says with that wide grin of his.

"Hi." Dev nods and smiles, aiming to look innocent, but he just looks guilty.

"What's going on?" Cam asks in his slow, friendly way.

"Nothing," Anika says.

Mick jumps at her, tail wagging. She ignores him, but Dev falls to his knees and reaches out to Mick. The dog gives Dev's hand a long lick then sits by him. His tail swishes as he gazes up at Dev with big, gentle eyes.

"I think your dog remembers me," Dev says as he strokes Mick. "I think your dog likes me."

"Sure, he does," Cam says. "So, what's up?" he asks Anika.

"We were digging for fossils, if you must know." Anika feels too awkward to meet Cam's eyes; she tries not to notice the muscles beneath his too-tight T-shirt.

Cam nods. "There's tons of fossils in Nova Scotia. I'll show you, if you like. There's lots in cliffs. You have to be careful though. The cliffs are unstable, they could crash down on you."

"It's okay. We'll find them ourselves." Anika doesn't mean to say it rudely, but that's how it comes out. She doesn't want to be friends with Cam. He is too cute. She can't help liking him, and her parents wouldn't want her to like a white boy.

Cam frowns. "'It's okay. We'll find them ourselves,'" he says, mimicking Anika's English accent. "I'm just being friendly," he tells her in his own voice. "These islands are public land."

Anika stares at Cam's hostile face and flushes.

"We're explorers." Dev looks up at Cam as he strokes Mick. "We're only used to cities. London especially. Everything's old there. But here, everything feels new and exciting."

"That's great, but you don't *own* this island," Cam tells Dev in a softer tone.

"We call it Kids' Island," Dev says.

Anika feels her cheeks heat. She wishes Dev wouldn't use that babyish name around Cam.

Cam nods. "Its real name is Wreck Island." He pauses a moment, glances at Anika as if wishing she'd be nicer, then turns to his dog. "Come on, Mick." And he walks away. Mick jumps up and follows him.

Dev sighs as he watches Cam leave. "I like him. And Mick."

He gets to his feet and turns to Anika. "He might take me in a boat."

Anika looks at her brother's sad face beneath his maple leaf hat. "Come on. Let's go. I'm hungry."

"Okay," Dev says. "But later, I'll find all the gold. I've got hungry eyes." And he stares at Anika, so hard his eyes bulge.

Anika chuckles. Dev *does* have hungry eyes. She is always busy in her own head. But Dev is slower and notices more.

"Come on then, Mr. Hungry Eyes," she tells him. "Dad's making chicken curry and I've got a Hungry Belly."

6: White as milk

Cam dreams he's in *Ashley* and it's evening, getting dark. Rough water is throwing his boat about, but Cam feels sure he'll be okay until a rogue wave arises. It comes from nowhere. It's just there, tall and terrifying, like a brick wall, a fist in the face. The wave soars over the boat, hard and determined as a hammer. It falls. And Cam falls, sunk by the wave's weight, into the darkness and frigid valleys of the ocean.

He jumps awake, heart drumming, and stares into the gloom of his bedroom. He sees the shadows and outlines of familiar furniture and objects, but his breath is still coming hard and his face is hot and slick with sweat. He breathes deep. *It's a dream, just a dream.*

He sits up, wishing his dad had never told him about the rogue wave hitting his fishing boat. Two crewmen were swept overboard, his dad said. One got trapped under the hull and almost drowned. That guy gave up fishing and has a land job now. Cam breathes deep again—his dad's story has got inside his head.

Then, he remembers John, and his stomach swirls with fresh alarm.

Knowing there's no way he'll get straight back to sleep, he climbs from bed and goes up to the kitchen, stepping carefully to avoid making the floor creak. He doesn't want to have to explain to his mom why he's wandering around in the night.

He gets a glass of water and a couple of chocolate chip cookies, then goes into the den, switching on a light to feel better. He drinks his water and chews on the cookies. He'd like to try one of the beers his dad left, but his mom likely knows how many are in the fridge.

The following day, he's still wound up about John, and he's worried about Anika and Dev, too. They are always on Wreck Island or the nearby beach. He's seen them walking about, and sunbathing too. Anika wore a bright green swimsuit. She was lying reading a book while Dev searched the sand. Cam had stared at Anika in her swimsuit then realized he was being a creep and hurried away, glad that she hadn't seen him.

But it's been a few days now and he needs to get back on his boat. Kevin has texted him about harvesting more rockweed. Cam has considered motoring down the coast for rockweed, but the rockweed off Wreck Island is especially good and there aren't many people about to see him. Just Anika and Dev.

Anika lingers in his mind as he puts his clothes on and gets ready to join his mom for breakfast. Anika is smart as well as pretty. It would be good to be friends, to get to know her better. But they haven't got off to a good start and he needs her out of the way.

He sighs as he walks up the stairs to the kitchen. He's not hungry, but he must sit with his mother and act nice. His mom needs his company.

She looks up from the table and beams at him as he enters the room. As soon as he sits down, she reaches across the table and takes his hand. "Cam, I want to tell you that I'm proud of you, and grateful for how you're handling...everything..." Her fingers knead his and she smiles into his eyes. "You're such a support, Cam. You're my rock."

Cam feels his cheeks heat, and his eyes dip to his coffee mug.

"Don't let John bother you, love," his mom says as she lets his hand go.

Cam says nothing, but his mom keeps saying that. It's weird the way she keeps repeating the same things. She can't have dementia, can she, like Robbie's gran? His mom must be too young for dementia. Or maybe she's too worried about money. Maybe she's losing her mind.

"If only your other friends were here," she says. "If only Neil and Robbie weren't hiking in Cape Breton."

"I'm fine," he says. "I'm not a kid." He picks up his toast and takes a bite. Anika's in his head again but he can't start liking her. She's a problem; a nuisance.

He wonders what his mom would think of him dating a dark-skinned girl. Has his mom ever been friends with someone of another race? It seems unlikely because their part of the province is so quiet and nearly everyone is of Scottish or European descent.

"It's very vanilla around here," one of his dad's friends once said.

"Yes," Cam's granddad had interjected, "And that's how I like it."

"Mom," Cam says now. "I met some new kids on Wreck Island. They're from London, England. They're not white."

"Really?" His mom raises a brow. "I hope people treat them better than they did me. When I moved here, lots of people made me feel an outsider because I'm Acadian and speak English with a French accent. Sometimes, when he was upset with me, your granddad would ask your dad why he didn't marry a local girl. Even now, after all this time, I still feel like a *come-from-away*."

Cam is surprised to hear all this. He studies his mom. He can't imagine her as a young girl, growing up speaking French, although he's visited her home and her parents in Moncton many times. It's impossible to imagine his mother's life without her being here, with him at the centre of it.

"You never told me Granddad was mean to you," he says.

She shrugs. "I wouldn't want you to be angry with your granddad."

Cam nods—that kindness is typical of his mom. She still speaks English with a soft curling accent.

He's never thought it marked her as an outsider. It just sounds like her unique way of talking.

"But Nova Scotia feels like home now, right?" he says.

She nods. "I like Nova Scotia but I do miss New Brunswick. I miss my parents and speaking French." She leans toward Cam, her eyes bright. "How about we move to Moncton, Cam—would you like to?"

Cam feels he should say, 'Sure, if you want to, Mom,' but he can't bring himself to. It would be bad enough to have to move to Halifax or Bedford, but Moncton? That would be...alien.

"Come on, Cam," his mother says. "Let's go. *Veux-tu m'accompagner à Moncton?*"

His mom stares at him then chuckles, a wide smile lifting her face. "Just teasing, Cam. But we might be making more trips to see your grandparents."

Cam grins and nods. "Sounds good."

He watches his mother sip her coffee, and recalls how his father used to laugh when his granddad talked about immigrants coming to steal jobs. His granddad always referred to newcomers as 'imports'.

"Those imports should go home," his grandfather had said once as they watched a TV news story about a Syrian family arriving in Nova Scotia.

"Granddad, they're refugees, not imports. Imports are things. These are people whose country has been destroyed," Cam said. "And I don't see a whole lot of immigrants rushing to take our jobs, Granddad. We're all white as milk around here. And there aren't many jobs."

His grandfather grinned. "Well, let's keep it that way," he said. "The fishing's bad enough with the rich folks buying our licenses. We don't need a bunch of foreigners coming in."

Cam's mom had looked over from the sink where she was washing dishes. "Grandpa, you like Alan," she said, referring to Cam's classmate who was half Korean.

"Oh, Alan's all right," his granddad said. "He can't help his slanty eyes."

Cam's dad had chuckled.

Infuriated with them both, Cam had slammed his mug down on the table. "You two know we're all immigrants, right? The native people are the original Canadians."

"*S e gille mì-mhodhail a th'annad,*" his grandfather said, turning to him with a scowl.

Cam didn't know much Gaelic but he knew enough to know his grandfather was calling him rude. His grandpa always reverted to his Scottish roots when he wanted to make a point, even though none of the family understood him.

Cam had said nothing, just got up and stomped down to his room where he had put Ashley MacIsaac's music on very loud.

Now, he frowns. His dad was wrong to encourage Granddad when he was being racist, but Cam misses his dad's laugh. *Dad was always joking around. Dad was fun. He was only ever really quiet and peaceful when he was fishing.*

"I've got to get going," he tells his mom, remembering that the tide is currently mid-way between its highest and lowest points. He can't harvest rock-weed or dulse between tides, but he can grab his fishing rod and head to Stony River.

At the river, he might be able to spot the special trout his dad saw. And fishing will make him remember the good, companionable times with his father. Standing by the water, a fishing rod in his hand, he might lose the feeling that his dad is a ghost, looming in the darkness of his mind, haunting him, laughing at him.

"I'm going fishing, Mom," he says.

"Okay," she says. "Be careful," she adds, same as she always does.

Cam nods, same as he always does, and goes to put on his rubber boots and get his fishing rod and a bucket of worms to use as bait.

Carol Moreira

7: What's a hundred years?

"What are you?" the man says.

"Pardon?" Anika doesn't know what the man standing before her is asking, but he is blocking the store's doorway so she can't ignore him. She recalls that Nova Scotians say 'pardon me' and not 'pardon', so she adds, "I'm sorry, pardon me?"

"You know…" The man smiles. He has that slow way of talking and his green eyes are bright with something—interest, curiosity? "What are you? Syrian? Korean? Indian?"

Anika's face flushes. "I'm British," she says. "Born and raised in London."

"You don't look British." The man puts his head on one side, seeming to doubt her. "Your English is good, though."

"They speak English in England," she says. "And not all British people are white."

He stares, then frowns; unease crosses his face.

Anika wishes she hadn't spoken so sharply. She trembles inside. The man likely didn't mean to be insulting. He's inquisitive, that's all. He's quite old and unfit-looking—maybe he eats too many of those awful Canadian doughnuts. His face is tanned and lined by the sun and wind, so perhaps he's a fisherman.

"I am of Indian descent," she says, not wanting to upset him, not wanting him to walk away and tell his friends there's a new, rude, dark-skinned girl in the village. She can't afford to upset people. She's a novelty, she stands out. She needs to be liked, to feel at home.

He nods. "Ah, that explains it." A grin brightens his face. "Welcome," he says.

"Thank you," Anika says, and smiles with relief.

"What are you doing here in Nova Scotia?"

"My parents have got jobs in Halifax." Anika warms with pride. "They're scientists, marine specialists."

He nods. "I hope they're not the kind of scientists that mess with the fishery."

Anika flushes. "No, no they're not." But her mother might be—her mother is looking into ways to improve the health and quality of farmed fish amid the impacts of climate change. But it's none of his business.

The man gives her a long slow nod, then turns and strides toward the counter. "Morning Sean," he says. "A pack of my usual smokes, please."

Anika opens the door and walks out into the sunshine. It's bright and warm, but she shivers and the bag carrying the two-litre container of milk feels heavy in her hand. Is she going to be a freak everywhere she goes in Nova Scotia? Sadness rises in her chest and tears fill her eyes. *That will be unbearable.*

I'm just a person, a person.

Angry with herself, she blinks hard. *Stop it, Anika, don't cry in the street.* But the tears remain. She doesn't want to be stared at all the time; she wants to fit in.

She stops walking, pauses to wipe her eyes, and the shopping bag swings against her legs. How quickly her thoughts and fears are spinning away. But she longs to run up to her questioner and tell him, *I am a British girl, a Londoner, of Indian descent, and that's all I want to be. That's what I am, and it's not so very different to you.*

She starts walking again, past the white-washed church that advises passers-by to *Discover the Fisher of Men.* The sign looks odd to her and she doesn't respond to its message. She longs for the familiarity of a Hindu temple. Is there one in Halifax? If not, even an English-style church or cathedral would do.

All the painted, wooden buildings look so new here, like they've just been built. Where is the history? Maybe, in Canada, the native people are the only ones with real history, the only ones who've been here for a real length of time. *It's probably just a hundred years or so since that church was built,* she thinks as she passes the neat little building. *What's a hundred years compared to the length of British history, of Indian history?*

She walks on down Bedford Lane, past an old shed, so wind-blasted it leans at an odd angle. It reminds Anika of a rhomboid diagram from math class. She moves past the clustering stone figures that act as a memorial to lost fishermen. The memorial shows fishermen setting off on their boat, watched by a mother and child on shore. The men on the boat look purposeful, but the family members are sombre, as if already anticipating the men's loss.

It's a very moving piece of art, and Anika has stood to admire it before but she doesn't connect with it today. *I don't belong here. No one in my family knows anything about making a living on the water. Mum studies the fishery, but she doesn't fish. We're not like these people.*

She hurries down the street. *I'll wear sunglasses, I'll hide.* Her eyes fill again as she thinks of her friends in London, friends whose ancestors came from all over the world. *It's okay,* she soothes herself. *It's okay. If you don't like it here, you can move back, go to London for university.*

But she still feels gloomy when she returns home. "Here's the milk, Dad," she says, dumping the bag on the counter.

"Thanks, love," her father says with a smile. "That's a great help."

Anika nods and notices how dark her dad's skin seems after all the white faces she's been looking at. The uniform darkness of her father's hair, eyes and skin is a contrast to the rainbow-coloured people all around. *I never used to notice such things. My own family never looked weird to me before.*

She feels angry with her father. Why did he agree to come here when her mum got that job? There are jobs in London. What will happen if she stays in

Canada? Will she be Canadian as well as British or will she stop being British? *No, I will not. I will always be a Londoner, always be Indian.*

"Dad," she says. "Will we stop being British if we stay here?"

He is opening the cupboard door, reaching for a mug. He is not looking at her, and she thinks he doesn't like the question. "No, Anika, of course not."

"But what if you like living in Nova Scotia, but I don't? What if Dev doesn't and I do, or Mum does and you don't?"

He pauses, his hand frozen around the mug. His other hand rubs his chin. "What exactly do you mean, love?"

"Well, the family might split up." Anika feels fresh tears rise and blinks hard. "It's bad enough that all our grandparents and cousins are in Kolkata and we hardly ever see them. It's good to be adventurous, Dad. But maybe we've been too adventurous?"

Her father stares at her; concern, softness, fill his face. "We will always do what's best for us as a family, Anika," he says, bringing his mug to the counter top. "And we see your grandparents and cousins as much as we can."

"But what if what's best for me is not best for Dev?" Anika insists. Her mind spins with all the awful possibilities. Her family could be dispersed, scattered like autumn leaves. Why is her dad being so slow to understand? He should have thought of this. Her parents are supposed to be smart, but they have not thought this through.

"Canada will give us—make us—*more*, not less," her dad says. "We'll become more...experienced, more international."

Anika stares at her father. She feels he is trying too hard to look and sound sincere. She glances down at Dev's dear little face—he has appeared out of nowhere, as he often does—and she sees love and confusion in his eyes.

She puts out her hand and strokes her brother's hair before looking up. "What if we all end up wanting different things, Dad—being different people, living different places?"

"Come here, honey." Her dad steps toward her.

But Anika's still angry. She feels bad for her father—she senses his own doubts about this move, she sees them in his face, which is sad, when he thinks no one is looking—but she backs away from him. "Come on, Dev," she says. "Let's go."

Dev puts his little hand in hers. "Let's go, Dev," she says again, and she leans down and kisses his soft cheek. She'd better look out for her brother. He needs her more than ever now their parents have been so reckless.

8: Creeped out

As Cam and Mick cross the road outside his house, wispy strands of sea mist still curl around the shoreline, and Cam smiles as that peaceful fishing feeling begins to slip into him.

When he reaches the place where Stony River narrows and empties into the ocean, he stops and opens his box of worms. He picks out a long fat, wriggling one and hooks it onto his line. Then he steps into the water and casts the line in the long, soaring arc his dad showed him when Cam was a kid. The line bobs in a yellow streak of sunlight, then sinks.

Cam settles down to wait. In school he can't sit still, but he can stand and wait for hours when he's fishing. His mind and body empty and focus on the water.

He loves the river. It starts far away inland, but it's home for the salmon who return to breed every year. It feels like home to him, too.

He sighs as he relaxes, realizing that harvesting rockweed and dulse have left him tired. His arms and legs are heavy and glad to rest.

Cam stands and watches as insects and air

bubbles break the water's surface. Sleek brown fish dart among the rocks and seaweed, but Cam sees no trout, not even ordinary ones. Several times his line grows heavy, but he knows it has merely snagged on submerged rocks and plants. When a trout has a line in its mouth, the line bends low in a way that's unmistakable. You feel the fish's life force on the other end; its will to escape.

When Cam hooks a fish, he usually lets it go. He likes to catch and eat fish, but it's even better to watch them swim away.

Time passes, and Mick falls asleep. He snores softly, his snout resting on his paw.

Maybe this is the wrong spot. But it can't be. He's watched trout swim up Stony River many times. And his dad said this is the place. His father wouldn't make a mistake about a thing like that.

Cam stays in the water. He doesn't want to leave without catching that special trout.

When he notices his feet are so cold he can't feel them any more, he begins to feel creeped out. Not creeped out like he would if he was swimming in the ocean and a shark fin sliced toward him, but uneasy. He feels as if someone is hiding in the nearby trees or on Wreck Island, watching him.

He hopes it isn't John. It's childish, but his friend's name—even the letters J - O - H - N—loom menacing in Cam's head.

He can't believe their dads had a fight. He can't believe he and John are fighting. His whole life they've been such good friends, hanging out in each other's homes, laughing, arguing, as relaxed with each other as family.

Cam stares at the trees on Wreck Island and tells himself John isn't hiding in the woods. No one is. He thinks about the movie he saw about a mountain climber whose toes developed frostbite. The guy's toes looked like black bits of barbecued sausage the way his dad cooks them. Cam tries to wiggle his toes warm, but his feet are so numb he can't be sure his toes are even moving.

He longs to climb out and stamp his feet warm, but doesn't want to scare the rainbow trout away. He wants the fish to come. He wants the fish to come more than he has ever wanted any fish. He stares into the water, willing it to appear, but sees only rocks and plants.

"Maybe it's the fish that's watching me." He can't lose the feeling of eyes on his face.

"Not catching much, O'Connell."

John.

Cam's heart accelerates with alarm. Cam's feet are in the water, but his heart is acting like he's running a marathon. He scans Wreck Island's shore, hoping John hasn't overheard him talking to himself.

"You're a crap fisherman—just like your dad and your granddad."

There. John is standing on Wreck Island among the trees. He's wearing running shorts and sneakers, a T-shirt that clings to his muscles. He's working out, getting fitter, growing stronger and more threatening.

Cam's face heats. "You and your dad are assholes," he yells.

"You're pathetic, midget," John says.

Cam watches John disappear among the trees. His peace has gone. Rage burns in his body, hot and simmering, like the embers of a campfire after the flames have gone.

He longs to call his father about John, question him about the fight with John's dad. But no. His dad is in Toronto. He barely bothers to text.

Cam will sort out his own problems.

9: Her pulse accelerates

On Wreck Island, Anika and Dev climb up to the highest point. From there, they see the sea and sky melded together in one fuzzy, heat-shimmering blue line. *It's beautiful here,* Anika reminds herself. *It's clean and lovely.* And she breathes deep into her chest and decides she will not worry about the future and create problems where maybe there aren't any.

"Come on, Dev," she says and she opens her backpack and pulls out their dad's tools. Against her better judgment, she has agreed to keep digging for the golden substance they found on the island, and they get busy picking gold from the earth and chipping it out of the big, grey rocks.

Dev isn't careful and some of his gold crumbles and falls on the ground, but Anika doesn't care because all around there is more gold than they can collect. Maybe this stuff is worth something. It might not be gold, but there could be valuable minerals.

Anika pauses as she sees their backpack is already nearly full. "We'd better take this batch home."

"What's up?" a voice asks and there's Cameron,

standing under a tree, his dog at his side.

"Nothing," Anika says, trying not to notice how her pulse accelerates at the sight of Cam.

"Mica's not gold," Cam says. "And neither's iron pyrite. They just look like it. Iron pyrite's called fools' gold."

Heat jumps in Anika's cheeks. She'd suspected this, and here she is making a fool of herself in front of Cam.

"It's just minerals," Cam says. He sounds apologetic, as if he doesn't like to disappoint them, but also a bit smug, like they should have known better. "They're everywhere in Nova Scotia."

Anika feels her hand jerk by her side. She wants to reach into the backpack and chuck a fistful of the worthless, glittering stuff at Cameron. Here's something else she hadn't known about Nova Scotia. And she had guessed—she'd thought it unlikely that Cam and other local people would just leave gold lying about. She's let Dev's enthusiasm and her own imagination— all those childhood stories about buried treasure— vanquish common sense.

She looks away from Cam to Dev. Her brother looks like he could cry.

"I'll get rid of this lot, then," Dev says. He reaches into his pockets and tosses handfuls of mica out.

Anika wishes Dev would stop. She doesn't want Cameron to see how much fake gold they've collected. "So...we're not rich." She shrugs and grins as if she really doesn't care.

Dev empties his pockets then bends to stroke

Mick. The dog wags his tail and circles Dev, rubbing his body into the little boy's legs. Dev runs his hand along the dog's rippling back. "I wish I had a dog," he says.

"Do you think your parents will get you one?" Cam asks. "I was about your age when my dad got Mick for me. I was so excited when my dad came home with him. 'Special delivery for Cameron O'Connell,' he said. It was awesome."

"I don't know. What do you think, Anika?" Dev turns to her. "Do you think they'd let me have a dog?"

Anika shrugs. "Maybe…" She glances about at the wild island. "This is a really good place to have a dog."

Dev nods. "Yes!"

"Well, if your parents don't agree, you can always spend time with Mick," Cam says. "Mick likes you. He likes you a lot."

"Thanks Cam!" Dev's face gleams.

Anika smiles and she feels herself soften toward Cam. Her eyes meet his. "Thank you," she says, and she feels a rush of happy affection for both her brother and this new Nova Scotian.

The fake gold doesn't matter— why did she think it did? "That's really kind of you, Cam."

Carol Moreira

10: What you got there?

Cam hasn't seen a single trout. He tells himself he should stop returning to the river. Once again, he's wasted his time.

He hasn't even felt close to his dad. He just stood in the river while his thoughts jumped about between his dad, John, and Anika—pretty, quick-talking Anika with her bright eyes—and the difficulty of harvesting rockweed now she's always around.

He turns and climbs from the water. As he walks up the bank, he hears an unusual tinkling sound, and looks along the river to the ocean's shore where there is a blue bottle lying against the rocks near the river's entrance. The ocean must have carried the bottle along and dumped it. The waves are pushing and rolling the bottle against the rocks, kneading it like his mom kneads dough with her rolling pin.

Cam pauses and contemplates walking over. The bottle might be worth adding to his collection. In the basement at home, he has ancient bits of water-smoothed sea glass, dented tankards and shards of plate. He has rusty keys, coins and fossils, chunky knobs of dinosaur bone and a calamite fern, beautifully outlined in rock.

This bottle could be attractive enough to sell on eBay. He's already sold some of his tide-pummelled treasures to raise money. He doesn't know what they're worth, whether or not they're real antiques, he just posts a photo and a buyer snaps the item up —or not.

He gazes down the shore at the bottle. It could be from a shipwreck, but it's likely just garbage. A lot of garbage washes up—empty water bottles, crushed and battered coffee cups. Plastic in all its horrible, garish forms snags on branches and skips crazily along the sand. Condoms too, used ones. The condoms look fat and white like some kind of rotting sea slug.

If this is plastic, he will pick it up. He often takes garbage home to dispose of, even the condoms. He keeps a pair of old gardening gloves in his pocket for handling those.

He sighs. Why are people so stupid? Plastic bags get swallowed by whales. Straws catch in turtles' guts. Cam fears that soon every living thing, including humans, will be choked by plastic.

He decides to see what this is and walks over. He picks the bottle up and turns it in his hands, noting how the pale blue colour is overlaid with crusty white stuff. Cam knows from experience the white stuff will be hard to remove. There is a faint white crest, like a crown, edged with swirly white lines.

He stares at the bottle and wonders who it belonged to. Maybe the owner was a long-ago immigrant, just arrived from Europe, or maybe the owner was lost at sea before they even arrived.

I'm lucky my own ancestors didn't drown, Cam thinks. *If they had, I wouldn't be here.* He shivers. If he'd never been born, would he be a ghost? Would he exist at all?

The bottle is interesting and maybe worth something. Cam is about to pocket it when he hears the voice of his former friend.

"What you got there?"

Cam turns. John is just a metre or two away. His T-shirt is dark with sweat, his face is red. He's been running.

"What you got there?" John stares at the bottle in Cam's hand.

"Nothing." Cam shoves the bottle deep in his pocket. It barely fits, and he feels the bottle as a tight swelling against his thigh. John's not getting it.

"Woof!" Mick jumps up and runs to John.

"Come here, Mick," Cam says.

Mick ignores him and Cam feels a hot burst of temper. When will Mick realize John isn't their friend anymore?

John doesn't look at Mick. He walks toward Cam.

Inside, Cam flinches. John's neck and jaw are so thick. Cam throws out his chest and stands straight. He will not look scared. John wants him scared.

"Give it to me, small fry." John holds out his hand.

"No!" Rage pulses in Cam, lends him the courage to stare back.

"Don't make me take it from you."

"You're not getting it," Cam says as John reaches out a huge hand and grabs his shoulder. "I said you're not getting it."

John tightens his grip, almost lifting Cam off his feet. His other hand comes in and jerks Cam back and forth. His hands grip Cam's shoulders, and Cam feels his head jump and swing. *I don't care what he does. It's mine.*

There's a growl. From the corner of his eye, Cam sees Mick leap forward and snap at John's ankles. Mick's hackles are up and he's growling, low and dangerous. Cam has never seen Mick so angry.

John twists toward Mick, although his hands remain around Cam's neck. Mick throws himself at John's right leg and his teeth snap around the hem of his shorts.

"What the...Get off, Mick!" John drops Cam.

Cam staggers backwards but manages to stay on his feet. He watches John swing his leg wide to loosen Mick, but Mick has a firm hold on John's shorts and won't be shaken off.

John swings his leg wider, but Mick refuses to let go. All four paws are off the ground. Cam sees Mick's teeth clamped around John's shorts as he spins.

"Get your mutt off me!" Panting, John gives up and stands still.

Mick bumps into John's legs as he slows. When he reaches the ground, Mick releases his grip.

John glares at Cam, his eyes fierce.

Cam glances at Mick. The dog is watching John. A low humming growl emerges from Mick's throat.

"You're not getting it," Cam says. The old bottle is likely just a piece of junk, but right now it seems the most important thing in the world.

John stares. "I don't want it anyway," he says with a downward glance at Mick. John's face is crimson and sweat beads in the hair above his lip.

Cam is relieved and surprised to see John looking beaten. "Okay, Mick, leave him."

Mick growls and seems to be gathering himself for a leap.

"I said *leave him, Mick*," Cam shouts.

Mick looks at Cam. He stops growling and backs away from John.

"Come on, boy." Cam bends and stretches out his hand. Mick runs to him, giving Cam's fingers a quick lick. "Let's go," Cam says, and he and Mick turn and walk up the beach.

"I'll get you, Cameron O'Connell," John shouts after them. "You stay away from here."

Cam doesn't look around. He's scared John might follow but he refuses to run. He walks. His heart hammers and sweat smears his face, but the fight is over.

His heart is still leaping when he steps under the trees that overhang the road and the nearby parking lot. A long furry caterpillar swings into his face and Cam steps out of the way and glares at the caterpillar as it bounces back up the thin white strand it's spun from its body. He sees that the caterpillar is trying to return to the safety of the branches.

Those things sure can jump. Still angry and

scared, Cam swings Mick's leash at the bug, breaking its safety harness. He's pleased to see it tumble helplessly to earth.

Mick runs ahead and grabs a stick. He turns to Cam, hoping Cam will throw the stick for him to fetch.

"No, Mick, leave it," Cam says with a scowl.

Then he feels bad for being mean to his dog and the bug. "Okay, then," he says. He takes the stick from between Mick's teeth and chucks it as hard as he can up the road. The stick arcs through the air, then hits the pavement, bounces and skids before halting. Cam smiles—that was a good, strong throw.

But as he watches Mick race toward the stick, he feels his sadness. *I'm a loser. It's pathetic to be 13 years old and so upset about losing your dad and fighting with a friend.*

11: Nerves spin her belly

Dev whoops and jumps when he sees the white sand sprinkled with sand dollars.

"It looks like a big hand threw them," he says. He stoops to pick a large sand dollar from the beach.

He turns it in his hand, admiring the starfish shape outlined on its shell. "Maybe it's God's hand that threw them," he says as he tucks the sand dollar away in his pocket. "Or Neptune's."

Anika grins at her brother. "Maybe."

She gazes at the beautiful beach and the nearby island's rocky shores, but today the lovely scene looks empty, lonely. Where are all the people?

Her thoughts turn to London and her best friends Tamara, Claire and Karen. She feels an ache in her chest. If only she could spend just a few hours with those girls who know her so well. If only they could chat and laugh in the sun.

She sighs and recalls running around Clapham Common with Karen. The big green space was always crowded with other runners, kids, and old folks all chatting and walking at different speeds, but it felt good because the park and people were part of her community.

Where will she train here—on the roads, on the beach? She's tried running on the beach but the sand drags at her feet, and it won't work when everything is covered in snow. Who will she train with? She can't always run alone.

She wonders if Cam runs. No, Cam isn't an option.

At least I've got Dev, she thinks as she watches her brother tuck sand dollars away in his pockets. In fact, Dev's with her almost every day. The only time she gets to herself is when she goes for a run or hides in her room to read.

"If you leave me behind, I'll tell Dad you're going to Kids' Island and the beach," Dev threatens and Anika believes him.

Their dad still doesn't know they go to the island almost every day. They tell him they're hanging out with kids and teens who live down the hill and he believes it. Anika is surprised their father accepts this story—he hasn't even asked the names of their new friends—but she figures he's too busy to think straight.

Right now, he's unpacking boxes that have arrived from London. When the boxes arrived, their dad looked tired and sad.

"You don't like Nova Scotia, Dad, do you?" Anika said.

"Of course, I do." He'd fixed a fake adult smile on his face. "But I miss my friends and London more than I expected." He gave his shoulders a funny shake. "I'll be okay once the semester starts."

Anika nodded. "I miss my London friends too. Nova Scotia's beautiful, but... lonely."

Her dad reached out and tousled her hair. "Let's keep our chins up, sweetheart," he said, and Anika stepped in and wrapped her arms around her father. He'd hugged her back for longer than usual, and she had the feeling he needed the embrace as much as she did.

Now Anika feels nerves spin her belly as she recalls her encounter with the man in the store. It's nearly September and that means it's almost time to start a new life at a Canadian high school. How different will a Canadian school be? She heard on TV that some Syrian refugee kids at a nearby school were bullied when they showed up at a soccer game. Those kids were trying to participate in their new country, and other kids yelled "Go home" at them. Anika had trembled at this news, and it reminded her of the story about the Black kid being harassed on a beach.

How will she cope if the other students hate her? Her parents should have got jobs in Vancouver. It would be great to live in that beautiful glass city on the Pacific. There are people of all races in Vancouver, in Toronto too. *We're not even in Halifax,* Anika thinks. *We're out here in the country with only white people. We'll have to drive into the city to find any food that's not burgers or fish and chips and chowder.*

She frowns, feeling as if someone is watching her. It's that feeling of eyes on the back of your head.

She spins around, assuming it's Cam. But it's not. It's a stranger—a guy, about Cam's age but taller and more muscular.

He stares at her. "Who are you? What are you doing here?" he says.

Anika stares back. She doesn't feel like answering his rude questions, but she remembers the man in the store. She doesn't want to make an enemy.

"I'm Anika. I've just moved here with my family from London in England," she says, remembering there is also a London in Canada.

"Well, go back to London. There's no jobs here for people like you." The boy's face swells with hostility. His eyes glare.

Anika steps away. She wants to challenge him, to say her parents already have jobs in Halifax, better jobs than this guy will ever have. *My mother's researching ways to help fish and fishermen, and my dad has a university job.* But the boy looks so intimidating that her words don't come.

She thinks again of the kid who was threatened with a noose. Is this guy going to attack her?

"Anika?" She turns to see Dev strolling up the beach toward them. She wants to tell her brother to run; her heart thumps at the thought of this thug attacking her little brother.

"Stay there, Dev," she says. She turns back to the scary guy. "We're just leaving," she tells him. And she walks toward her brother, wraps her hand around his shoulder and leads him away.

"Who's that?" Dev asks as they walk back across

the sand. He turns, craning his neck to look at the stranger. "And why are we going home already?"

"I don't know who he is," Anika says. "And I'm tired. I want to go."

For once, Dev doesn't argue. As they walk, Anika thinks how this is all their mum's fault. Their mum was the one who first got a job in Halifax and then insisted they live in a village out of town because she wanted "old-fashioned family values and healthy living" for Anika and Dev.

"It'll be wonderful," their mum had said with a big smile. "Don't expect the worst."

Anika frowns. That's easy for her mum to say when she isn't threatened and treated like a weirdo everywhere she goes. It's easy for her mum to say when she won't be the only non-white teen in school. Easy for her mum to say when she's a respected scientist.

Who is that big bully, anyway? She glances over her shoulder and sees him striding along the beach toward the village.

Cam says the islands are public lands. That kid doesn't own the beach either. Should she ask Cam who he is? Her frown deepens. She should have been nicer to Cam.

"Look, Anika." Dev points and gazes up at her. "There's Cam and Mick."

Anika looks down the beach and sees Cam up ahead. He is picking things out of the sand and putting them in a bag slung from one hand. Mick sits nearby.

"Maybe he's collecting sand dollars like me," Dev says. "I'm going to shout and wave."

"No," Anika says. "Don't, Dev. I don't feel like talking right now."

She blinks as tears threaten. *I'll never feel at home here,* she thinks. *Never.*

Dev's lip juts. "But I like Cam and Mick."

Anika nods. "I know."

She begins to feel angry about the bully. How dare he treat her like that? He has no right to scare her, make her stay away from the beach and the islands. She won't be imprisoned in the house.

She puts her shoulders back. No. She had enough of being locked up in a building during the pandemic. "Let's go back to the island and see what we can find," she says.

Dev grins. "Yes!" And they turn toward Wreck Island.

The tide is out and the sun is hot as they climb over the rocks that surround the island. Bugs bite their arms and legs, and when they reach the interior, Dev insists they stop for a break in the tent Anika made from her old dress. Anika agrees and crawls under the pink material with him.

Inside, she lies back and closes her eyes. She listens to seagulls calling and insects buzzing and tries to forget the bully.

But Dev soon gets fidgety. "My legs are stiff," he says and he crawls out into the sunshine.

There's more room without him and Anika stretches out. The sun shimmers through the cloth and warms her closed eyelids. She can hear the putt-putt of a small boat out in the bay.

The loud rat-tat-tat of a woodpecker starts up nearby. The sound knocks and rings in the silence. Anika feels sorry for the bugs hiding inside that tree —that woodpecker sure sounds determined to drill through the bark and get to them.

She must have fallen asleep because she's startled to hear Dev call her name. Then his face appears beneath the pink dress.

"There's black things," he says. "Black things in the water."

"What black things?"

"I don't know." He frowns. "Come on."

Anika crawls out and follows him. Dev drops to the ground and begins creeping along on his hands and knees. Anika guesses he's trying to hide from the black things, whatever they are.

She copies him, although she feels stupid crawling across the island. She hopes no one can see her and glances nervously at the bushes as they crawl along. It would be embarrassing if Cameron appeared with Mick.

But there's no one about. The island is still and quiet. Soon, they reach the seaward side and crouch behind a blue-grey rock.

"Look!" Dev points to a group of six dark circles bobbing in the water.

Anika thinks the circles might be seals. Maybe the black things are a Canadian sea animal she's not heard of. Black bears and coyotes can be dangerous.

Whatever these are, she hopes the animals can't walk on land because they're getting closer.

She and Dev watch the shapes move through the water toward the long, white slope of the beach. Anika glances around, trying to work out how to escape if necessary.

Then she sees air tanks and other equipment heaped on the sand and a cool wave of relief rushes through her. "They're divers, Dev," she whispers. "They're scuba divers, silly."

Dev scowls. "*You* didn't know."

That's true. Anika's mood dips. There's so much she doesn't know about Canada.

She watches the divers wade onto the sand where the river meets the ocean. They look funny waddling up the beach in their tight, black wet suits.

But scuba diving looks cool. Maybe she'll give it a try. It would be amazing—beautiful—to see the world, the fishes and plants, under the water.

"There's Cameron again!" Dev says. Cam is walking toward the river. He's holding a fishing rod, Mick trotting beside him.

"He's going fishing," Dev says. "I'm going to wave," and he jumps up before Anika can stop him.

"No, Dev!" Anika grabs her brother's legs and drags him to the ground.

"Ow—that hurt!" Dev rubs his leg, tears brighten his eyes. "Why can't I wave?"

"You just can't," Anika mutters, although she does feel bad for Dev.

She feels bad for herself, too. She likes Cam. She

doesn't care about his scruffy clothes—she's becoming less interested in wearing the right brand of clothing herself.

"Come on, Dev," she says. "The gold was fake but there might be other cool things to find."

"I want to find things that make me rich," Dev says with a scowl. "And that's because I need to buy a boat and sail away from you."

12: His dad caught the bug

Cam frowns when he sees Dev's red baseball cap pop up and drop down behind the island's rocks. Now they're spying on him. Why does he like that girl so much when she's such a nuisance? How can he get rid of her? He needs to get back to the rock-weed.

He scowls as he returns to his fishing and stares down into Stony River. *Where is the rainbow trout?*

Cam has texted his father, and his dad actually replied. He said life in Toronto is going well. He's making good tips in the bar although he misses Nova Scotia and the ocean.

"Ontarians think lakes are as good as oceans," his dad texted. He had added an emoji of a shocked face. His dad said he would return to Halifax for a visit when he'd saved enough money to pay down his debt.

Cam smiled to think of his father dealing with customers in Toronto. His dad must be a good barman. He's funny, with an easy smile.

Probably I should chat more to the tourists at the restaurant, Cam thinks, *I'd make better tips.* Cam is polite to visitors when he clears away their dirty dishes. He tries to smile and act cheerful, but he can't pretend that all he ever wanted was to bring the tourists fish and chips and listen to them chat about the amazing views.

He doesn't much like the tourists. He resents the way they talk about the bay, his home, like it's some kind of beautiful theme park, and not a real place with real people living their lives. They say everything is "cute" and "lovely".

Cam's mom says they likely don't realize they're being rude. *Probably I should feel sorry for them. They have to waste their whole lives in stinking cities.*

Now his frown deepens as he recalls the rest of his dad's text. His dad had said *Ashley* and the ATV will have to be sold—soon. There's a strong market for ATVs.

When Cam received the text, he'd stared at his dad's words, his eyes lingering on the long-anticipated but unwelcome news. He still hopes his own money will be enough to save *Ashley*. The ATV is precious, too, because it's a link to fun times in the back woods with his dad and granddad.

Cam settles down to wait for the prized fish his dad saw. Again, the fish doesn't come. Only a few ordinary brown trout swim around.

Cam wonders about listening to the music on his phone. Ashley MacIsaac's fierce energy might lift him, but fiddling isn't fishing music and he doesn't want distractions. He fears John striding around a dune or leaping out from behind a tree. Even with

Mick there to protect him, Cam feels jumpy.

He thinks of Anika and recalls how he caught her and Dev collecting fool's gold. How can he get them off the island so he can get back to collecting rockweed?

Slowly, an idea forms in his mind. He'll tell them a story about treasure buried on Shadow Island, the one at the far end of the beach. Buried treasure is childish, obviously, but Anika is new in Nova Scotia and might just fall for it. After all, his own granddad was crazy about buried treasure. And his dad caught the bug, too, when the fishing got bad.

Cam frowns again. Should he bury fake treasure for them to find? He could hide some of the old stuff his mom has put aside to throw out, like the gold-coloured candlesticks and cups she bought from The Dollar Store. If Cam dirties the stuff up it could look old and valuable.

But no, that would take more time than he can spare. Anika would likely never fall for the treasure hoax anyway—she's smart; he sees it in her bright eyes, in the way she looks at him like she's deciding what she thinks of him.

What *does* she think of him? He flushes and pushes the thought away.

"Come on, Mick. Wake up, let's go," Cam says. He climbs from the water.

But Mick doesn't open his eyes. He just twitches his paw, deep in a dream. "Come on, Mick," Cam says. "Let's go."

He bends to shake Mick, and there's that tinkling

sound again. Cam glances along the seashore and sees something shiny bumping against the rocks. Walking over, he sees a large metal spoon lying among shards of broken plate.

Cam picks the spoon up and turns it in his fingers. It has a deep scoop, like his mom's soup ladle. It isn't as rusty as some of the other stuff he's found. This spoon is shiny and there's a faded blue and gold pattern on the handle. It's pretty. Cam decides to give it to his mom for her birthday, which is only a few weeks away.

As he turns for home, he sees a couple of planks of wood drifting down the shore. He puts the ladle in his pocket and walks into the water to retrieve the planks.

In his bare hands, they feel waterlogged, so heavy the water seems to be forcing the swollen wood fibres apart. One of the planks has a golden swirling crest on it. Cam guesses it's probably the symbol for the British crown. It's too indistinct for him to be sure, but it's interesting.

He decides to take the plank home. Maybe the crest will be easier to decipher when it's dried out.

He kneels to the plank, lifts the swollen wedge of wood. It's weird how ancient items are washing up so much more than in the past. Maybe there really is treasure, maybe the tide is washing it out of its hiding place. He feels his heart quicken. Could his granddad and dad have been right? He stands, the sodden wood in his hand. His dad left his metal detector in the garage. Maybe when he's harvested more rockweed, he'll check it out. It seems daft, but he has nothing to lose.

Carol Moreira

13: A dark thought

"There *is* real treasure you could look for," Cameron says. "There's treasure on Shadow Island, over there." He points down the coast. Anika feels skeptical but finds herself turning to look.

"Hundreds of years ago, pirates were chasing a ship from Spain during a big storm. The ship ran onto rocks and sank," Cam says. "Some of the sailors escaped in a rowboat with some of the treasure the ship was carrying. They came ashore on Shadow Island and buried it. The pirates caught the sailors, but the sailors wouldn't reveal where the treasure was buried, even though they were tortured. The pirates couldn't find it. No one has."

Cam pauses. Anika notices his face has turned red.

"It's been hundreds of years," Cam continues. He looks away from her eyes and glances down the shore to where a bird circles over Shadow Island. "Look, there's an osprey," he says. "Ospreys are cool birds. They build their nests in the same place for generations. See it?"

Anika and Dev watch the bird drifting above the trees.

"Why are you telling us about the treasure?" Anika turns back to him. "Why don't *you* look for it yourself?"

"Oh, I've tried," Cam says. "But I've never had any luck. Maybe you can share the treasure with me, if you find it."

Anika stares at the osprey flying above Shadow Island. She looks down at her brother. He is crouched by Mick's side, happily stroking the dog.

"Well, thanks for the story," she says. "It was very entertaining. Come on Dev." And she turns and walks away.

She doesn't trust Cam—he was red-faced the whole time he was telling his tale and he barely looked her in the eye. But she might check out Shadow Island.

Maybe that big, bullying guy doesn't go to Shadow Island. Twice over the last few days, Anika has seen the big guy striding along the beach, and each time she's turned around or hidden from him. He won't see her again if she sees him first.

Back home, their dad is still unpacking. "Come on, Anika. I need your help," he says.

Anika scowls. *Will it never end?*

Her father is standing in the kitchen doorway, holding yet another box of stuff from England. Her eyes move to the window, her thoughts turn to Shadow Island and Cam's story.

"Dad, give me a break," she says. "It's gorgeous out."

Her father places the box on the breakfast bar.

"Come on, Anika. I don't enjoy unpacking either. But it has to be done." And he goes back upstairs.

Anika sighs and tears open the box. It contains her books from England. She's glad to see favourite titles from way back, like *Harry Potter* and *Vampirates,* books she's outgrown but can't let go. She will put them upstairs, next to the blue cloth flowers she's placed in a vase as part of a shrine to the Hindu god Shiva.

Anika had smiled and relaxed as she sat before the blue statue of the dancing god. She isn't sure she believes in Shiva or any other Hindu gods—not literally, although it's possible they are all just different aspects of the one life that everybody, everything, shares. That's what her mother says, anyway.

Whatever, it feels important to keep her family's traditions alive in this new place.

As she unpacks, the urge to get to Shadow Island grows. There could be something there. Anika has read online about the pirates, smugglers and rum-runners who used to conduct their dark business around Nova Scotia's tiny bays and inlets. Even in modern times people have died searching for treasure on famous Oak Island, farther along the shore.

The stories about Oak Island made Anika shudder. There are secret tunnels and shafts there. Treasure-hunters have dug into them but the tunnels flooded, trapping the fortune-seekers. Equipment that worked just fine in other places inexplicably stopped working on Oak Island.

Some people say the island is haunted, even

cursed. Anika had frowned as she read—that's silly. Still, she wouldn't go searching Oak Island, but it might be worth checking around Shadow Island's trees, especially the ancient and battered ones. She is smart. She can spot clues.

She thinks of all the little islands in Nova Scotia. A drive along the South Shore reveals lots of pleasure boats bobbing in the water. Do some of those owners smuggle goods into the province, like their ancestors did? Maybe, especially now the fishing has gotten bad. People might smuggle in drugs, alcohol.

It's a disconcerting thought that things might not be as pretty and innocent as they look, but London isn't really tourist-brochure perfect either. Crime is a problem in London—Anika's parents always insisted she was home before dark, that they knew where she was and who she was with. *Maybe nowhere is exactly what it seems.*

"Hurry up, Dev," she says. Her brother is sitting on the floor, leafing through an old book on dinosaurs. "I'll go without you."

Instantly, Dev puts the book down and gets on with unpacking.

When they've finished, they find their dad arranging family photos on the living room windowsill. Anika feels another surge of homesickness when she sees a picture of herself and Dev standing outside their house in London. She thinks about the many shows and concerts she attended in London—Zoe and the Cool Cats was a recent great experience in Hyde Park. It felt wonderful to be part of that crowd of thousands of excited Londoners, especially after the pandemic had shown them all how bad it felt to not see a single friend, much less a crowd, for weeks on end. At the concert, It had felt like everyone in the city was your friend.

The memory makes tears cloud Anika's eyes, but she reminds herself she needn't lose touch with her old friends. *You're not on Mars, and Claire is already saving her money to come visit.*

"I bet it was good to see that old dinosaur book again," their dad says to Dev. "Are you looking forward to school, son?"

"*School?*" Dev's mouth swings open. "But Nova Scotia is a vacation."

Their dad smiles. "You have to go to school, son." He ruffles Dev's hair. "*Even* in Nova Scotia."

Dev frowns. "Dad," he says. "At school, will there be other kids like me?"

"What do you mean?"

Anika watches their dad's face—she's sure he knows exactly what Dev means.

Dev glances down at his arm that rests on the table. "You know, Dad. Other brown boys, boys like me."

"There might not be boys exactly like you, Dev. But there will be lots of children for you to be friends with," their dad says. He sounds like he's trying to convince himself. "And if there's no one exactly like you, that makes you even more special."

"Yes," Anika agrees. "That's right, Dev." But she frowns inwardly. Even her little brother is worried about not fitting in. *They'd better not bully Dev. They'll have me to deal with.*

Dev, reassured, nods and grins. "Please can we go outside now, Dad?" he asks as he makes for the door.

Their father shrugs. "Looks like you already are. Go on then. And take care. No going in the ocean. I mean it, Anika. You and Dev are not used to the water. None of us are. We all have to adapt and be careful now we're here."

Anika notes her dad's cautious words and despondent tone. She hopes he's not angry with their mother for getting the Halifax job.

A dark thought floats in from somewhere. Maybe her parents will get divorced, like so many of her friends' parents in London.

Anika's mind begins to spin with horrible images of herself and Dev shuttling between her parents' homes. *Where would we live? Would we stay here, or go back to London? To our grandparents in Kolkata? What if Mum was here and Dad was somewhere else?*

She tries to shove the worries from her mind. She can't, she won't, think of it—not her parents.

And she won't talk to her dad about the bully on the beach or the racists in the news. She doesn't want to worry him any more than he already is.

14: Doesn't matter what they call it

Cam grins as he walks home. Anika won't be able to resist searching Shadow Island. The fiery curiosity in her brown eyes told him that.

He walks into the garage and his nostrils fill with the smell of old fish coming from his father's boxes of fishing tackle. The scent reminds Cam of all the times his dad came in from the ocean smelling of fish and salt water.

In the corner, there's the old outboard motor he and his dad once spent an entire summer taking apart and putting back together. Good times. Gone now.

Hungry, he goes into the kitchen to grab a ham and cheese sandwich.

"Is that you, Cam?" his mom shouts from upstairs.

"Yup," Cam yells back. *Who else would it be?*

"Get yourself a sandwich, love."

"Okay." Cam wonders why his mom always tells him to do what he's just about to do. He makes the sandwich and gets a Coke from the fridge.

"Come on," he whispers to Mick who is lapping noisily from his water bowl.

He grabs his backpack and sets off, Mick trotting beside him. As he walks, Cam thinks about his dad's fishing boxes and his own battered wooden sled lying nearby. He remembers the day his parents took him on a sled ride. The sled was pulled by huskies. The huskies were beautiful but tough. They kept fighting over which of them should be lead dog in the harness. For most of the ride a dog called Ice led, but a younger animal, Beavertail, kept nipping at Ice's legs. In the end, the musher switched the two of them around.

"That's the way huskies are," the musher told Cam. "Keen to work and just as keen to fight over who's boss."

Cam feels sadness catch his throat. He hadn't realized how happy he had been that day. He'd been young, of course, and he couldn't have known life could change so fast.

There's no sign of Anika and Dev or anyone else on the beach or on the shore of Wreck Island. Maybe Anika's already on Shadow Island. Pleased, he strides toward Wreck Island's rocky far shore. He grins as he sees *Ashley*, still moored nearby, and the rockweed floating on the water. He can't wait to get started.

But as he strides over the island, he feels his phone vibrate in his pocket. It's a text from Kevin:

Sorry Cam, I can't take your rockweed anymore—people asking questions about my harvester's age.

Cam feels his feet slow. He stops, his belly swirling. *John. Has John alerted people, the cops maybe?*

The thought makes him hot with fury, and he's also sad, heavy.

He reaches the island's shore and sits on the edge of the cliff that overlooks the bay. He stays there for a long time, his feet dangling over the rocks and water. He stares at *Ashley*, sitting idle on the waves, with the rockweed lying like a floating carpet all around.

He sighs. Well, that's that, then. His most lucrative source of income—gone.

He raises his face to the warming sun and feels despair prickle behind his eyelids. *We'll never keep the house now. We'll have no money.* He blinks hard and sits longer, until, surprised by a cooling breeze on his face, he stares out at the ocean.

Long, white-cap waves are moving toward land. Maybe bad weather is coming. He realizes it's the first time he doesn't have to worry about his dad being caught in a storm. His dad can't drown in Toronto. Cam and his mom will never have to be the bereaved family at one of those church services where the community prays for lost fishermen. *We have lost Dad, but not in the way we feared.*

He thinks of his father and the friend his dad lost long ago. They'd been part of a crew fishing for lobster and his dad's friend fell overboard and drowned. The weather wasn't bad that day but the crew didn't notice the man go over. They were busy with the ropes and the nets, and the roar of the boat's engine filled their ears.

The tragedy haunts Cam's dad. "I didn't see him fall, Cam," his dad told him once. "By the time we realized, it was too late. The ocean looked empty. We searched and searched. It was getting dark."

Cam hated seeing that sadness cloud his dad's usually merry eyes. Fishermen are brave. Most people who eat fish probably never think of the people who catch their food, who risk their lives on the ocean.

He watches the white-cap waves hurry to shore. The sky is filling with clouds shaped like mackerel fins. It's likely just a passing squall, but the weather is changing. Cam sighs. It's easy to lose important things, it's easy to lose people.

"Come on Mick, let's go."

As he gets to his feet, he sees John walking along the beach near Stony River. John looks like he's searching for something. Cam thinks of the blue bottle he found there and wonders if anything new might have washed up. He resolves to go back and check the shoreline. He can't harvest rockweed any more, but he has time to explore with his dad's metal detector. John will not keep him away. John doesn't own this place.

As he walks in the door, he sees his mom's anxious face. "Cam, thank goodness you're here!" his mother says. "There's a tropical storm coming. It's heading straight for us. Can you help me get the chairs and plants off the deck? The storm will be here by to-morrow."

"A tropical storm?" Cam says. "Do you mean a hur-ricane?"

"They're calling it a tropical storm," his mom says.

"It doesn't matter what they call it—it's a big one."

Cameron nods and frowns. "Okay." He hopes the storm won't damage the dulse. If it does, he won't even have *that* to harvest.

Carol Moreira

15: My hat!

Anika grabs her backpack from beside the door. She's packed two apples and two apple drinks along with a shovel and trowel. She figures she and Dev can last all afternoon if they have to.

Outside, they walk down their long, paved driveway, cross the narrow country road, and turn right onto the beach. Despite the dragging effect of the sand on her feet, Anika speeds up, wanting to get to Shadow Island as fast as possible. She doesn't believe in lost treasure, and yet the thought of it is pulling her.

"Hurry, Dev," she says. He's already beginning to slow.

"I *am* hurrying," Dev says.

Anika sighs as she feels the sun's heat scorch her face. It never gets this hot in London. Her backpack grows heavy, her feet too.

She's relieved when they reach Shadow Island, but is shocked to find that the sand causeway between the island and the beach is hidden beneath ankle-deep, swirling water.

Dev takes one look at the whirling water and

backs up the beach. "The causeway's disappeared," he says, seemingly unable to believe his eyes.

"It's okay, Dev." Anika tests the water with her bare foot, watches it swirl about her toes. "We can get through. I bet I can touch the bottom with my toes all the way across."

"But it's wilder, deeper, than it's ever been."

"It'll be okay. I'll help you."

Dev sighs. "If I yell, you better save me."

"Of course, I will," Anika says. "I'd never let you drown."

But Dev doesn't yell. Once he's in the water, he concentrates on swimming and keeping close behind Anika as she pushes out to the island.

She reaches it without difficulty. Then, clambering up the rocks, she turns and looks at her brother as he puts out his hand and grabs for the safety of a rock. Dev's face is pale and Anika realizes he's genuinely scared. She feels guilty.

"Good job, Dev," she says as she bends to pull him from the water. "You did it. You're brave."

"Brave and stupid are different, Anika," Dev says. He stands, shivering, the water rushing from his body. "Sometimes you're stupid."

"I am not," Anika says, although she thinks maybe Dev is right. In this new Canadian world, she can't always tell if she is being adventurous or foolish or even if she is happy and free or lonely and sad.

"Come on," she says, and she leads Dev to the seaward side. She thinks the long-ago sailors who buried the treasure would probably have chosen the seaward side as the ocean is wilder and more dangerous there.

It feels uncomfortable walking across the island. The seawater trickles down their legs, their clothes stick to their bodies and the sea salt begins to dry and scratch their skin. When they reach the island's far side, they get another shock. The ocean is surging against the rocks. Huge waves are cresting in and banging against the coast, flinging up glittering spray.

"These rocks look mean as shark teeth," Dev shouts above the wind. "Anika, I don't like it..."

He slaps his hand to his head as the wind lifts his maple leaf sunhat. Too late. The hat is gone. "My hat!" he shouts.

"It's okay, Dev. I'll get you another one. Let's hurry." Anika raises her voice against the wind. "Now, Dev, look for a tree that might have treasure buried under it. Remember, the treasure's *old* so it must be buried under an *old* tree."

Dev stares at the few scrappy trees. They are skinny and twisted and leaning at strange angles. They've obviously been pushed and shoved by the wind forever.

"That one." He points to an especially thin, bendy tree. The tree's branching roots stick like skinny fingers through the thin soil.

Anika shakes her head. "No, we can see its roots so we know there's no treasure underneath."

"That one?" Dev points to a tree with a sturdier trunk.

They walk toward it as the wind increases, arcing the tree backwards.

Dev wipes his nose with his sleeve. "The wind is making my nose and eyes run." He stares at the clouds racing across the sky. "I can't see any seagulls, Anika. Even the birds are scared."

The wind whips Anika's hair into her eyes. "Don't worry, Dev," she says, although she is beginning to feel worried about the weather. The anxiety is like a tiny worm burrowing against her brain, which keeps telling her everything is okay.

Dev watches the trees bowing in the wind. "It's getting wilder."

Anika frowns. "Okay. Let's go."

She and Dev hurry toward the side of the island that faces the beach. It's a relief to approach the rocks and trees on that calmer side. But Dev, who has run ahead, yells, "Oh no!"

It *is* frightening. The ocean is bubbling in the space between the island and the beach. The water is spilling over the island's shores and more water is pouring in all the time. Anika has never seen water like this and fear begins to spin her belly.

"Call Dad!" Dev says.

Anika frowns. "I can't."

"You forgot your phone?" Dev's voice rises in terror. "Anika! What will we do?"

"I'll swim over and get help. You wait here." Anika tries to keep her mind and voice calm.

"No, the water's too crazy." Dev gazes at the whirling, sucking ocean.

"Don't worry," Anika says as she crouches down. She eases her backpack from her body and drops it on the rocks, then lowers her legs into the sea.

At once, she realizes she can no longer touch the bottom with her feet. She looks at the beach. It's not far away, but the water between is high and churning. She has no choice though—she must swim for help. She lets herself go, and sinks into the ocean.

Anika is such a strong swimmer she manages well—at first. But, about half-way across, she feels new currents pulling at her legs. It feels as if the currents are trying to drag her in different directions. Waves keep submerging her head. Each time the water ducks her, she comes up coughing, her mouth full of salt water.

It gets worse. She tries to kick straight for the beach but is pushed to the right. The sea is shoving her back, around the island. She will be swept away.

"Anika, you're not swimming straight!" Dev yells.

Anika tells herself not to panic. Panicking is the worst thing she could do. In England, when her class teacher was mean to Anika for a whole semester, Anika got so scared she couldn't go in the teacher's classroom without her stomach rolling like the ocean is now. She mustn't get scared like that.

Instead, she kicks for shore, but the little control she has is diminishing fast. *I'm going to drown,* she thinks.

But she can't believe it. She won't believe it. She kicks harder.

16: Approach from downwind

Cam stares at the little book in his hands. He's read Sir Jeremiah Stamford's personal diary before, but there's something about the age of it— the diary is for the year 1814-1815—that still amazes him. It makes him pause and take his time. And now it's his —he *owns* Sir Jeremiah's diary.

It's been a weird day. Cam's mom came up to him in a hushed, solemn kind of way and said that his grandfather's will had been read and the old man had left Cam the diary. Now, the slim, brown, leathery book filled with Sir Stamford's spidery writing is resting between Cam's own living, sun-tanned fingers.

Filled with an anxious, pulsing energy, Cam gets up to stretch his legs. He's already re-read the diary once in hopes of spotting clues his granddad and father may have missed. He found nothing except Sir Stamford's records of ordinary things like the building work on his house and brief accounts of his privateering expeditions along the eastern seaboard: *captured the Boston clipper, seized ten cases of wine, five cases of tobacco, ten of flour, 20 of sugar, 30 mus-*

kets and 10 chests of silver.

Cam wonders about the violence of the expeditions. He hopes the American crews made it safely back to the U.S. He decides to ask his mom about the diary and finds her in the kitchen baking peanut butter squares.

"Mom, how did Granddad get Sir Stamford's diary?" Cam asks, sitting down at the breakfast bar and dipping his finger into the tub of peanut butter.

"Cam." His mother frowns. "Use a spoon. And don't get peanut butter on the diary."

"I won't," Cam says in a muffled sort of way, around the peanut butter.

She glances at the window; outside the sky is darkening. "I want to get this lot baked before the storm arrives, in case we lose power.' She looks back at the book. "Your granddad probably found the diary at one of the auctions he loved to visit before he got sick."

Cam nods. "Granddad must have been amazed when he realized it was Sir Stamford's diary. The personal diary of a bad-ass schooner captain. Wow."

He looks down at the little book on the breakfast bar. "Do you think the auctioneer recognized the name Sir Jeremiah Stamford? I'm thinking he couldn't have or the diary would have been too expensive for Granddad to buy."

His mom shrugs as she lifts a teaspoon of peanut mixture onto the baking tray. "Most people are forgotten soon after they die, Cam."

"Most people, yes," Cam agrees. "But not Sir Stamford. I can't believe I own it now. It's awesome."

His mom smiles. "It is good to have it, I'm sure. It probably makes you feel closer to your grandfather. But don't *you* go crazy about treasure-hunting, like your dad and granddad did."

"No," Cam says.

"They were too...imaginative, irrational, at times," his mom says.

Cam scowls. He hates it when his mom criticizes his father. "Granddad and Dad likely just hoped to find the treasure and surprise us all," he says. "They wanted us to be happy, to have no money worries."

"Maybe," his mom says as she slips the baking tray into the oven.

Cam looks down, stares at the diary. His grandfather didn't find any treasure, neither did his dad. Cam has never believed in the treasure. He used to agree with his mom that it was a fool's errand, but he's getting more and more keen to get out there. The idea is taking hold of him. If there *is* treasure out there, this could be his turn, his chance.

Is this how obsessions and addictions start, he wonders—with people believing that their luck has changed, that they're fated for something big?

He goes down to his basement bedroom and checks on eBay. He grins. The items he posted for sale last week have made him $600.

It's hard to part with the things he finds, but the money is great. And if people are prepared to pay so much, then obviously people who know more than he does must think the items he finds on the shore are valuable.

He picks up his iPad and googles *metal detectors, gold.* The detector his dad bought on Kijiji is lightweight and folds away neatly in his backpack, but it's not very powerful and that might be why his dad never found anything on Wreck Island.

Cam scans several sites and discovers he might need a two-box detector. If the gold is buried deeper than one metre, a regular metal detector might not find it. He sighs. The stronger detectors cost hundreds of dollars, even used ones. He has the money, but he needs it for helping his mom with the bills, for trying to save *Ashley.* Should he spend it? It's a big risk.

His eyes slide to what remains of his collection of beach treasures arranged along a shelf. What should he sell next? The crusty bottle he recently found is standing tall among an assortment of old coins. The ladle isn't there. Cam has hidden it away and is going to clean it up to give to his mom for her birthday. She will smile when she opens it.

He hears the wind slap against the house. It's been thumping against the window for a while. He moored *Ashley* off his wharf, then pulled her ashore and tied her to a tree, but maybe he should move her farther inland.

Then he has another thought. Maybe Anika and Dev are out there right now, investigating his story about buried treasure on the other island.

The idea flips his belly. What if they didn't hear the weather report? *If they're out there, it's my fault,*

I told them to search Shadow Island.

He gets up and walks to the window. He lifts it softly so his mom won't hear and swings himself up onto the windowsill.

"No Mick," he says, turning to his dog who's padded over behind him. "You stay here where it's safe."

Mick whimpers as Cam crawls out of the window. As he stands up, the wind pushes Cam's chest. It feels like someone is shoving him and he thinks of John. But he puts his ex-friend out of his mind and manages to slide the window shut.

He runs to the water with the rain smacking his face. The wind seems to be forcing him back. The wildness is frightening, but exhilarating. The air is full of salt. It's like the wind and water have become the same. Cam breathes deep, feeling the buzz of the storm's energy. The world is electric.

Cam reaches *Ashley* where she lies tied to a tree up from the water. He unties the rope, then leans in to pull out his life vest. He slips the vest over his head then walks to *Ashley's* stern and begins to drag her back down the sandy shore toward the water. His sweat is mixed with rain and salt water by the time he finally gets *Ashley* to the wharf and pushes her out onto the water that is already churning and slapping against the shore.

Quickly, he plants his hands on the boat and pulls himself up and in. Clambering to his feet, he makes for the control panel and switches on the engine.

His boat usually roars to life when he turns the key. The engine noise fills the air like it means business. Now he can feel the engine's energy trembling beneath his fingers on the wheel, but he can't hear the motor above the surging wind. Even when he rams his foot down on the throttle, his boat struggles to move away from the dock.

As he inches out into the bay, Cam feels like he's forcing *Ashley* along with the power of his mind. He grips the wheel between his hands and tries to hold her steady, but his boat rocks and spins in the waves.

Eventually, she rounds the headland past Wreck Island and travels on toward Shadow Island. By sea, the route is longer than on foot and it seems very long now. Cam is cold and scared. His clothes are soaked and cling to his body.

"Come on, girl," he urges his boat. He pats the wheel as if *Ashley* is an animal he can encourage. "Come on."

He's careful as he circles Shadow island. Hitting a rock would be bad. Even a small hole in his boat would be serious in waves like these.

At first, he doesn't recognize the red thing he sees floating on the water. Then his heart lurches against his ribs—it's Dev's maple leaf hat.

Cam scans the water. "Dev?" he shouts.

There's no reply and nothing to see except massive waves rushing in and bursting on the island's rocks. Cam shudders. He longs to turn back, but he must check the landward side.

He urges *Ashley* toward the churning patch of water between the island and the shore, still talking to her as if she is alive. "Come on, girl, you can do it," he tells her.

When he sees Anika's head in the ocean, he doesn't realize what it is. Her dark hair looks like the tip of a water-covered rock. Then he hears Dev shout. "Cam, get Anika!"

Cam spins toward Dev's voice and sees the little boy standing on Shadow Island. Dev is pointing at the rock.

Cam's pulse jumps. "Anika!" he yells. But she can't hear him. His voice is faint, weakened by the roar of the wind. She doesn't turn. Her head is getting lower in the waves.

Cam's dad once told him that you should only approach people in the water from downwind because it's easier to control a boat's speed with the bow heading into the wind. So he gets himself downwind of Anika. He turns off his engine, watches her, and steadies *Ashley.* He tries to judge the motions of the waves and his boat.

He can see Anika's arms making useless swimming motions. He wants to reach out and grab one of her hands, but he can't hold the boat steady. The waves are shoving the boat toward her. He's terrified the hull will slide over her head and push her under.

He realizes there's a tiny window of time when the boat approaches Anika and is then pulled back by the current. He must reach down and grab her as the boat rolls back.

Anika is getting ever lower in the water. Her head is sinking, her arms barely moving. She's obviously exhausted. Cam must grab her. He counts in his head, timing the seconds as the boat approaches Anika and then swings back with the waves. Four seconds. He has just four seconds to get her out.

One, two…He braces his legs against the boat and leans down to grab Anika's arm. He catches her sleeve, but the water pushes her forward and his fingers scrape along her back.

He lunges. Down. But his fingers merely scrape her body.

Again, he lunges. This time, his fingers close tight around her arm. A grin of relief lifts his mouth. *I've got her!*

17: Crazy for treasure

Anika watches Dev shout and point, but all she can hear is the hissing whoosh of water. Her body is heavy. She won't be able to keep her head up much longer.

She fixes her eyes on Dev. If only she could be standing beside him on the island. If only she'd never insisted they swim out. She's a fool. Her little brother has more sense than she does, and now she's going to lose him and everyone else for ever.

Something grips her arm. She twists in the water. Cameron is in his motorboat. She sees the yellow of his life vest. He is shouting at her. He pulls on her arms. He is trying to haul her out.

Hope lifts Anika and she manages to get hold of the boat's edge. She tries to lift herself up but her arms are weak and she keeps tumbling back. Then she feels Cameron's fingers tighten around her arms, and she rises from the ocean. She pitches forward, tumbling onto the boat's floor, water rolling all around, as Cam swings *Ashley* about and makes for the island.

When they get close, Cam holds the boat steady

under the point where Dev is standing. "Jump," he tells Dev.

Dev hesitates.

"Jump!" Cam yells.

Dev turns and grabs Anika's backpack from the rocks. Then he jumps. The boat rocks as he drops in beside Anika. He clutches onto his sister, leaning against her body.

Anika holds him tight. Tears fill her eyes. She feels Dev's body shaking. She's shaking too.

Cameron turns the boat toward the community. *Ashley* bucks in the waves and the wind blasts their faces, but they manage to inch closer to the cluster of houses. When they are close enough, Cam leaps from the boat. He holds *Ashley* steady while Anika and Dev climb out and stagger up the beach. Then Cam hauls his boat up the sand.

As soon as he has secured *Ashley*, he turns to Anika. "What are you doing out here? Don't you know there's a tropical storm coming?" he shouts against the wind.

Anika frowns. "We didn't know." She wriggles her toes. It's a relief to feel the beach beneath her feet. A giant shiver trembles through her body, but she breathes deep and tries to look calm. She doesn't want Cam to know how scared she's been. She's messed up, big time.

"Thank you, Cam," she says. Cam's face is pale and his wet clothes stick to him. Anika sees he's been scared too. She feels bad for putting them all in danger and glances up the beach toward home.

Dev gazes at Cam, a look of adoration on his face. "Thank you, Cameron," he says. And he reaches out and wraps his little arms around Cam's waist, resting his head against Cam's belly. "You're a hero."

Cam colours up. "Thanks Dev, but I'm no hero." He pats Cam's back, a little awkwardly. "You get home now, little guy."

Cam turns toward his boat. Anika watches him drag the boat back down to the water. Cam is strong. And brave.

She looks away and shivers as she tries to wring ocean water from her shorts and T-shirt. Then, she glances up the beach, toward their new house and her father's warm arms. She takes her backpack from her brother and takes his hand in hers. "Come on, Dev. Let's get home."

As she speaks, she realizes it's the first time she's thought of the sprawling Canadian house with its wide windows and decks as home.

Once inside, Anika isn't surprised to find their father crazy with worry.

"Where have you been?" he demands as they come in the door. "I've been looking everywhere for you. Your mum called; she's on her way home. There's a huge storm coming. Why are you so wet, Anika? You're soaked."

"We were on the beach," Anika says. "The waves rushed up. I fell."

She glances at Dev—he'd better not say anything, but for once her brother stands mute. Anika tries to look normal, although her stomach is churning with the sea water she's swallowed. She wishes she could tell her dad that she nearly drowned. She needs another long, comforting hug from her father.

Her dad frowns. "Go and get out of those wet clothes, both of you. I told you to stay away from the water."

Anika slips upstairs. If she stays out of her dad's way, he'll soon forget about being upset with her.

Sure enough, by the time Anika comes down, their dad has made mugs of hot chocolate. He brings them down to Anika and Dev in the basement. "I'll be relieved when your mum is safely home," he says.

The storm hits in the night. Anika wakes, startled by the wind howling outside her window. It sounds horrible. The storm thumps around the house. Anika lies in bed and tells herself she absolutely is not scared.

In the darkness, she can see the shadows of the heaving branches outside her window and the dark shapes of her furniture. Her favourite books are arranged on the shelf, along with the medals and certificates she won in track and field events. It feels good to have her things around her.

Her thoughts turn again to the upcoming semester. Will she be alone in the new school? Will Cam be her friend? The thought of his kind, handsome face makes her smile into the darkness. A deep warmth fills her entire body.

But why would Cam want to be her friend? He won't. And she can't blame him.

She shudders, the thought of being alone at school

is more frightening than the storm. And she must stop liking Cam. It just won't work with her family. Her parents will expect her to meet a Hindu boy in Halifax, and preferably not until university. That's what they did. They waited for each other.

Still, she wonders what she looks like to Cam. He can't be used to dark-skinned girls. Does he like the way she looks? Maybe she just looks weird to him.

The following afternoon, Anika is surprised when Cameron comes to their house.

"Anika and Dev, you have a visitor," their father says as he leads Cam into the kitchen.

Anika smiles. "Hello." She aims to look friendly, welcoming, but feels her temperature rise, a warmth in her cheeks. She glances at her dad, fearing he might have seen and interpreted her blush, but her father is beaming at Cam.

"Hi." Cameron greets them all with a wide grin. "I was bored with being inside, although I guess we're lucky at our house—we still have power."

"Our lights went out in the storm," Dev says. "I drank all the orange juice before it got warm in the fridge."

"Is it safe to go out now?" their dad asks. Anika watches her father. What does he think of Cam? Does he like him?

Cam nods. "It's safe. The wind's dropped a lot. I thought Anika and Dev could come to my house. I live on the next street, Blueberry Hill."

"That's kind of you," their dad says. Anika smiles. She sees that their father is happy Cam's asked them round. Cam is cool, the way he knows about the weather and everything.

Her dad must see that Cam is a good, smart guy. It doesn't matter that he's white and working class.

Dev turns to Cameron. "Do you want to see my sand dollar collection, Cam?"

"Sure, that'd be great," Cam says, and he and Anika follow Dev into the garage where he has arranged his most prized sand dollars on a shelf.

"Great specimens," Cam says as he picks up and examines Dev's treasures. "You've got some amazing ones, Dev—some of the best I've seen."

Dev's face turns shiny with happiness.

"Do you want to see *my* collection of treasures?" Cam asks him. "I've got all kinds of stuff in my basement—old bowls and spoons from wrecked ships, dinosaur bones, coins..."

"Dinosaur bones!" Dev claps his hands.

Anika grins. Cam is even kinder, more fun, than she realized.

She finds it interesting to walk down the hill and see the damage the storm has done. The wind has uprooted many trees. The branches and leaves are sprawled across the road and slumped on drooping power lines. That seems sad, but intriguing—she has never seen weather create such an impact. The wind is still strong and wild and Anika likes feeling it push against her body and through her hair.

"Thanks again for saving us, Cam," she says. Can she erase Cam's bad first impression of her? After all, he came to their house. He can't dislike her that much.

"Yes, thanks for saving us, Cam!" Dev says, and he walks even closer to Cameron.

Cam reddens. "It's okay," he mumbles. Anika notes the blush. *Cam is so modest.*

His house is right on the shore. When they arrive, Mick barks, but then he remembers that he knows Anika and Dev and his tail wags so hard it swings his whole body. He walks around them, pushing himself into their legs. Anika kneels to stroke him. He feels incredibly soft.

Cameron's mom comes out to say hello then she and Cam go back in the house and fetch peanut butter squares and Coke, with milk for Dev. "Isn't the weather thrilling?" she says as she puts the tray with the food on the deck. "Make sure you don't go near the ocean though. The water's still too high. Just sit on the deck and watch the waves."

They sit on the big wooden deck on a piece of damp tarpaulin and gaze at the ocean.

"The sea looks like it's sighing," Dev says as the waves rise and sink. "It looks like the storm's worn the water out."

"The ocean's often quiet after a storm," Cam says.

"I think all the energy's used up," Dev says.

"It's kind of nice how you two are always together," Cam says, looking back and forth between Anika and Dev. "It must be good to have a brother or sister."

"It's an Indian thing, partly," Anika says. "I mean the closeness. Family's very important to us."

Cam nods. "Family is important. I've realized that lately."

Anika doesn't know how to respond. She almost asks what has made him realize this, but that seems nosy, so she changes the subject. "I went online. This whole area is supposed to be full of buried treasure," she says.

Cam nods. "My grandfather was crazy for treasure stories, my dad too. Granddad was obsessed with Sir Jeremiah Stamford. He was a privateer for the British king during the War of 1812. Stamford got rich pirating American ships. He built a house on Wreck Island."

"That's cool," Anika says. "But where's his house?"

"Burned down," Cam says. "Maybe in revenge. My grandfather always suspected Stamford stole from the king. Someone found old records and there was a discrepancy between the amount of gold bullion Stamford took from a captured U.S. ship in 1814 and the amount he gave to the king. Granddad thought Stamford probably buried the gold on his own island."

Cam grins. "I found a plank with the British crown on it. It was just lying on the shore. I've caught the treasure bug. Finding that plank felt like a clue."

"Wow!" Dev says. He frowns. "Are privateers like pirates?"

Cam nods. "Kinda. They were legal pirates. The king gave privateers permission to rob Americans. The Brits feared the Americans would take Canada from them so they tried to stop the Americans trading with Europe and getting rich. The privateers stole whatever they could—muskets, gunpowder, gold, silver, jewellery—"

"But maybe Sir Stamford hid his gold somewhere else," Anika interrupts. "Maybe he took it to England?"

"No," Cam says. "Sir Stamford died during a battle with an American clipper in 1815. He never made it back to England."

There's a silence. They all gaze at the ocean and then around the deck, as if expecting to see Sir Stamford's treasure lying there.

"I'm going to look for it," Cam says. "My dad walked all over the island with a metal detector. He found nothing. I might get a more powerful detector. But it's expensive. I'll have a go with my dad's first."

"That's awesome!" Dev says. "Can I have a go, too?"

Cam nods. "Sure."

He glances away, his eyes flit over the ocean. He clears his throat. "Anika, Dev—I owe you an apology. I tricked you, telling you there's treasure on Shadow Island. I mean, lots of people think there is. But I don't. I just wanted you off Wreck Island because of Sir Stamford's treasure, and..." He doesn't end the sentence; maybe he doesn't need to tell them about illegally harvesting rockweed.

Anika frowns. She'd been suspicious of that story of Cam's. She should have listened to her doubts.

"I'm sorry," Cam repeats. His face reddens. "I feel really bad you got caught in the storm."

Anika sighs, remembering her own insistence on swimming in the threatening water. "Well, you did rescue us," she says.

Dev nods. "Yes!"

"So, you'll forgive me?"

"Yes!" Anika says quickly. "Of course."

Cam's eyes light up. "Thanks. Then maybe we can work on this treasure thing together. Because something interesting is happening. Ancient things keep appearing along the shore by Stony River. There's always been stuff washed up, but now there's much more. I think maybe big waves are breaking up a wreck and the tides are spreading the sunken objects about. There's wrecks all around Nova Scotia."

Dev's eyes grow big. "Ghost ships," he whispers.

"I've been collecting things I find on the shore," Cam says. "I've sold some of them on eBay." He grins. "I don't know how old they are so I just call them 'antique'. I was pissed when someone bought something from me for $50 and sold it on for $300. Some of this stuff's obviously valuable."

"Maybe it belongs in a museum," Anika says.

Cam nods. "Maybe. But my parents have split, and my Dad's in Toronto. We need the money. And in Nova Scotia, treasure-hunters can keep the treasure they find. Well, you're supposed to show it to marine archaeologists so they can put the best stuff in museums. But, like I said, we need the money." Cam sighs, juts his chin. "We have to sell our house."

Dev's lip quivers and he stretches out his hand and touches Cam's arm. "I don't want you to move.

You're our friend. We'll help you look for things along the shore. We'll help you make money. Won't we, Anika?"

"Of course," she says.

"Thanks." Cameron glances at Anika and a faint redness spreads across his cheeks.

Anika wonders what the blush means. Could he like her, too? She feels her pulse accelerate. *Could he?*

18: A survey of rocks

Cam has decided to use his dad's metal detector around the ruins of Sir Jeremiah Stamford's old house. As he studies the crumbling foundation, Cam wonders what Sir Stamford was like. He was a pirate for the English king so he must have been fierce and brave. *It would be cool to be that kind of fearless person*, Cam thinks as he checks over his shoulder for John.

Finding himself alone, he pulls the detector and spade from his backpack, opens them up and gets to work.

He walks slowly around the foundation of the long-ago home. It's hard to imagine this rubble was once part of a fancy house. *There used to be more money in Nova Scotia*, Cam thinks. There was shipbuilding, bootlegging, lots of fishing. It's hard to imagine those days, hard to imagine how the bay looked back when local people had money and more options.

He searches for dips in the earth that might suggest a sunken cellar or collapsed well. The detector does not beep and the remnants of Sir Stamford's house seem to mock him. Cam can almost hear John's voice in his mind: 'You're weird, just like your dad and granddad.'

After a while, though, the alarm on the detector sounds in Cam's ears and he feels hope spark like lightning through his body. The detector is beeping, chirping through his headphones. Something interesting lies in the ground at Cameron's feet and the detector doesn't want him to miss it.

Cam lays the detector aside and grabs his spade. With the spade's tip, he makes a small, neat cut in the ground, then kneels to lift the grass-topped section of soil. He peers down. Nothing. He scrabbles in the earth and finds two loonies. He holds them between his muddy fingers. They're bronze, dulled by burial, but modern coins, for sure.

He sighs, stands, and glares at the ground. Then he drags his sweaty hands along his shorts. His back aches. His throat is as dusty as a dirt road in a heat wave.

He kneels, replaces the plug of earth and grass, then stands and stamps on it to ensure a tight fit so the grass will grow back. Despite the disappointment with the loonies, he feels a kind of excitement, a hope, inside. He will keep searching for Sir Stamford's treasure.

Is this how Dad felt? he wonders. There's the fear you're wasting your time, but the hope won't die?

He picks up the detector and walks on over the island, slowly swinging the long, thin instrument over the grass and around the rocks and boulders. He ensures the sensitive transmitter coil covers as much earth as possible. He imagines the magnetic field that surrounds the coil reaching down through the thick soil, helping him.

"Hi Cam." It's Dev's piping young voice. Cam feels his lips twitch into a grin as he turns and sees the intent way Dev is staring at the metal detector.

"Hi, Cam."

Anika. Cam feels his temperature rise. "Hi, Anika."

She looks intently at him but he can't figure out the message in her eyes, so he turns to her brother. "Would you like a go with the metal detector, Dev?"

He feels glad for a distraction from the sight of Anika, who is wearing navy shorts and a red T-shirt. She looks amazing.

"Yes, please!" Dev skips forward, and Cam shows him how to hold the detector, how to sweep it over the area you want to search.

Dev becomes calm and still. *He's focused*, Cam thinks, *and he loves nature. He'd make a good fisherman.*

Dev walks up and down with the detector, and every now and then, the machine beeps. Then Cam digs and investigates, feeling fresh hope.

But he finds nothing except garbage—old buckles, tin cans, nails, more modern coins. Once again, he recalls his father's sense of failure.

He's surprised that Dev does not seem disappointed. The little guy exclaims over every find, almost as if it's real treasure. "Wow, look at this. I wonder how old this is," he keeps saying.

Cam finds himself grinning. His eyes meet Anika's. She smiles too; her eyes shine. It feels like they are sharing a secret joke, a secret joy. They don't have to say anything; their eyes speak.

The next day, when he's searching on his own, Cam is starting to think he'll have to tidy up the grass and go home when his spade clinks on something solid. There *is* something here—something hard.

He digs deep, then shoves the earth and sand away. His fingers reveal the outline of a rectangular wooden box. He grips one of the handles and hauls the box from the earth.

"It *looks* like a treasure chest," Cam says, and Mick comes over and gives the box a good sniff.

Cam gazes at the mud-crusted handles and the padlock holding the lid in place. He pulls a screwdriver from his backpack and tries to lever the lid open, but it won't budge. The padlock looks old and rusty, but it's tough.

Irritation prickles over Cam's skin. He's going to have to drag the box back to his house and use his dad's tools on it. "Okay, come on Mick."

He sighs as he bends to lift the box and is relieved to find it isn't too heavy. "Let's get going."

Back home, Cam forces the lid and the padlock gives way and flies into the air, landing with a clunk in a far corner of the garage. Cam yanks up the loose lid. Inside is a smooth, neatly arranged blue sheet. Cam pulls it off.

Disappointment streams through him. The chest is full to bursting, but not with anything valuable.

Kneeling down, he pulls out a thick blue binder. The label on it reads *Wreck Island, 1985, geological survey.*

"Rocks," Cam says heavily. Great—a survey of rocks.

He rummages deeper in the chest and finds a stack of papers held together by a green rubber band. *Beach River School 1980 student enrolment,* the label reads.

Rifling around a bit more, Cam finds a video of a movie, *Ghostbusters.* On the cover, a fat, happy-looking white ghost is trying to break out of a red circle.

"Why make a time capsule and fill it with boring, useless stuff?" Cam says, and he throws the thick video to one side. He stares into the box and sees a pair of eyes staring up at him. He jumps then realizes he's looking at a photograph.

Something about the eyes is familiar and he pulls the photo out from under the movie.

It's John! Cam's heart skips. *What is a picture of John doing in this box?*

Then he realizes it isn't John, although the boy in the picture has the same blond hair and strong jaw as Cam's former friend. The name under the face reads Alan Pierce. John's last name is Pierce and his dad is Alan.

Cam stares at the young face in the photo. Could this kid really be John's dad? John's dad is bald and fat, but it must be him. In 1980, Alan Pierce would have been just a boy.

Cam feels a sudden memory of shared laughter, and a wave of longing for the happy times he's spent hanging out at John's house. John's dad used to take John and Cam camping and canoeing in the summer. How has this stupid argument taken away all their history? Money, of course, money and fishing.

He wonders if the box might contain a picture of his own dad. He searches, and sure enough, he finds a photo of his own father.

Cam gazes at the shot. How could that smooth, freckly face be his wrinkly, sunburned dad? It is, though. The blue eyes are just like Cam's own eyes.

His dad's name is written under the picture, too—Angus O'Connell. *This stuff is a kind of treasure,* Cam thinks, *but it's not worth money. It won't help me and Mom stay in our house. It won't help me keep Ashley.*

He swallows hard and looks around the garage for somewhere to hide the box. The garage is full of his family's stuff. There's his dad's toolbox and gardening spades, the fishing tackle boxes, the outboard motor, the bicycle Cam got for his tenth birthday and his baseball bat, soccer balls and basketballs. His head dips—he is surrounded by ghosts.

He puts the lid back on the box and closes it. He's glad he's found the time capsule. He feels his mouth lift in a grin. He is surprised to feel happy—it feels good to have the picture of his dad.

19: It could die

"Anika, there's a baby deer lying on the grass. It's all alone. Is it okay?" Dev's face is creased with concern as he turns from the kitchen window and gazes at his sister.

"Show me," Anika says. She puts her phone down and gets up. She's not worried. The fawn's mother is bound to be close by. She smiles to think how she is already getting used to seeing families of deer grazing and resting in the backyard. Deer mothers are always near their young.

But Dev is right. Anika sees through the window a tiny deer lying all alone in the middle of the lawn. The deer is so small and so well camouflaged that Anika can barely distinguish the tiny body from the tall grass and the dandelions and bits of leaf and twig lying everywhere. The fawn is covered in white spots and patterns that blend into the garden. But she can see its little head sticking up, looking about, atop its slender neck.

"Its mother will be back soon," Anika says, hiding the prickle of concern she feels. "We should probably leave the baby—the fawn—alone so we don't scare the mother away."

"Okay." Dev frowns. "But it's so hot out there, too hot for a baby deer, maybe. I hope the mother isn't long."

Anika nods. She wishes her father were home so she could ask him what to do, but their dad has driven into Halifax to talk to his future colleagues at the university. Their father had smiled and seemed excited as he left the house. He was wearing smart jeans and a white shirt and blue tie, and he had shaved—he hadn't shaved in a while.

Dad's bored and lonely, Anika thought. *I'm not the only one missing London.*

"Come away, Dev," she says. "Let's leave the fawn alone. You want to play a game?"

Dev *always* wants to play a game. They play *Stone Warriors* until Dev gets up and moves to the window to check on the fawn.

"Anika!" Dev's voice trembles. "The baby deer has put its head down. Anika, come see!"

Anika hurries to the window. The fawn's head is resting on the grass as if it is too heavy to hold up. Is the fawn weakening in the heat? The little body is now barely visible. If they hadn't known it was there, they would likely miss it.

"Where's its mother?" Dev's voice rises with distress. "Why is its mum taking so long?"

"Maybe she's searching for food." Anika's eyes scan the trees and bushes at the back of the yard. *Where is the mother?*

"Let's go out there," Dev says. "We must. The fawn

might be injured. It might have been attacked. It could die."

Anika studies the tiny patch of white spots and brown fur lying in the grass. She feels a familiar uncertainty rise within her. She doesn't know what to do in Canada. She doesn't know about wild animals. She is only used to domestic pets.

"Okay," she says. "Let's approach it very slowly, very carefully, just to see if it's okay. No touching it, Dev, no scaring it."

Dev nods. "Course not."

"Follow me," Anika says.

She opens the back door and leads Dev toward the yard. She thinks that if they approach the fawn from behind, it won't see them. They will be able to check if it's okay without alarming it.

She walks slowly down the deck stairs and toward the tiny bundle of fur on the grass. Dev follows. Anika is pleased with how quiet Dev is being. Who'd have thought Dev could make so little noise?

But the deer somehow hears them. It raises its head, its tiny pointed ears twitch up, and it gets awkwardly to its feet.

Anika puts out her hand, cautions Dev to stop. They are still a few paces from the fawn. Maybe it will settle down again.

But Dev steps on a piece of summer-dried leaf. The small, crunching sound makes the deer startle and it moves swiftly across the grass toward the bushes and trees that lead to neighbouring gardens.

"Oh no." Dev's voice is so full of sorrow that Anika

pulls him in for a hug.

"It's okay, Dev. Look, the fawn is moving just fine. It's young, its legs are wobbly, but it's not injured. It'll be okay."

"But how will its mother find it now?" A frown puckers Dev's forehead. "The fawn will be all alone. It will be scared when it gets dark."

"I'm sure its mother will find it," Anika says as the fawn disappears from view.

But she isn't sure. Back in the house, she googles 'fawns left alone' and finds that mother deer often leave newborns because they're not strong enough to keep up with their moms while they feed and they risk falling victim to predators. The mothers return at dusk to feed the fawns and move them to safety. The only time humans should get involved is if a fawn is walking around and crying.

Anika frowns. The fawn hadn't been walking or crying. It had been lying still until they scared it away. A fawn has the best chance of surviving when it's with its mother, she reads.

Anika's heart sinks at this news. She glances at Dev. He is absorbed in a game on his laptop.

Quickly, she clicks on a link and listens to the sound of a young deer crying. It's a sad and haunting sound. It makes all the hair on Anika's arms stand up. A fawn's cry sounds strangely like the cry of a human baby. *If we hear that sound outside, it'll mean it's calling for its mother. That would be good—the mother might hear.*

Still, Anika's mind and body are filled with heaviness. *We shouldn't have gone out there. Why didn't I google it before? I think I'm so smart.*

She sinks her head to her hand. *I will never get used to Nova Scotia. In Canada, I act like a fool.*

20: The flow of water

Cam sits on his bed and passes his eyes once again over Sir Stamford's hard-to-read handwriting. Impatience stirs in his belly. Is he wasting his time re-reading the privateer's diary? Probably, but he has to continue.

He hasn't been able to buy the kind of high-power metal detector he needs from Kijiji. As soon as one comes up for sale, it's gone for more money than Cam has. Who knew so many people wanted metal detectors? There must be loads of people searching for something. What are all those people looking for?

Cam pauses, his eyes caught by a diary entry he has not noticed before. Under 15 October 1815, Sir Stamford has written: *went to the cold cellar and stocked it.*

Cam feels his pulse quicken. Why would Sir Stamford, a rich man who must have had servants, take things to a cold cellar? Maybe, just maybe, Sir Stamford hid treasure in the cold cellar.

Cam puts the book down on the bed. He gets up and strides about the room. Where could Sir Stamford's cold cellar be? Could it be under the ruined foundation Cam has examined so many times, or somewhere else on the island? Maybe even on another island or along the shore? Obviously, there was no refrigeration back in 1815. People used ice and cold water to keep food and drink cool. Cam's own dad told him how he's often kept Coke cold in a snowbank.

"It's a wonderful, Canadian way to keep drinks cool," his dad said. "You get to sit on the snowbank in the sun with a lovely cold drink. It's heaven. You've got to try it, son."

Cam keeps pacing. Too excited to stay inside, he calls Mick and together they walk to Wreck Island and make straight for Sir Stamford's home. Cam walks all around the foundation of the privateer's dwelling but doesn't feel the spark of new ideas. If only the house hadn't burned down. If only there was a proper ruin.

He steps this way, that way, his eyes darting, desperate for any clue. He hopes to see the outline of steps, steps that might lead down to an old cellar, something significant that he might have missed before.

But there's nothing. The remnants of the house look exactly as they always have.

He stops pacing and glances down at Mick, who's lying nearby watching him with his head cocked. The dog looks puzzled, as if Cam is behaving like someone else.

I am, Cam thinks, *I'm becoming crazy for treasure.*

"What do you think, Mick?" he asks. "Where is it,

boy? Where is the cold cellar?"

Mick gazes at Cam then he woofs as if trying to be helpful. Cam walks over and bends to stroke his pet. "I know, old boy. I'm losing my mind, aren't I?"

Standing up, he spins slowly, letting his eyes roam the island, then walks to the wilder, seaward side. He stands, gazing at the waves moving in from the ocean beyond the bay. He watches the waves as they hit the island's rocky shore. They send up spangles of spray before subsiding and drifting with the current across the island and toward the beach where Stony River empties into the ocean.

Cam watches the flow of water and an idea begins to form. The idea is so indistinct and dark he feels it is something lost and he's grasping for it. Then his mind finds the idea.

A cave.

Cam has been gathering objects, bits of broken plate, planks, along the shore. Maybe the current is carrying things from a hidden cave on the seaward side of the island?

It isn't a crazy idea. There are lots of sea caves in Nova Scotia. Images of other sea caves he's seen and visited fill Cam's mind. It might even make sense.

He looks back down the shore toward Stony River, and there is John. His former friend is kneeling, about to pluck something from the sand.

Cam ducks down so John won't see him. His heart thumps at the sight of his friend-turned-enemy, and, as he glances at the rocky island coast beneath his feet, his heart spins harder. He doesn't want to dive down there into the cold and the dark, with the wild waves and currents all around. It's dangerous.

But he's going to do it. He is.

Maybe he'll ask Anika to help, to keep watch from *Ashley.*

21: That vivid, secret world

Cam sits in *Ashley*, waiting for Anika and Dev. As he looks at Stony River and the shore, a shiver wriggles up his back. He frowns and scans the shoreline and the trees—he doesn't need any more trouble from John.

His instinct is to hide away but he sits straighter then reaches out and turns on his music. Brisk fiddling fills the air and he smiles, tapping his foot, feeling the sounds lift him. John can't say where he can and can't go.

Still, he yells at Anika and Dev to hurry when he sees them strolling down the beach. They run, then wade through the clear water and clamber aboard.

"This is exciting," Anika says, as she stands, wringing seawater from her shorts. Her shorts today are purple. Cam glances away.

"*Ashley*'s a weird name for a boat," Anika says, glancing down at *Ashley*'s bow where the name is written in curly black lettering.

Cam grins. "My boat's named for Ashley MacIsaac. He's an awesome Nova Scotia fiddler. That's the music you're listening to right now."

Anika pauses and listens, a grin spreads across her face. "I love this music. It's wild."

Anika's smile is bright. It lights her eyes. She sits down on the padded chair behind Cam's seat, and Dev sits next to her.

"Scottish people were some of the founders of Nova Scotia," Cam says. "Nova Scotia is Latin for New Scotland. And the French were founders, too. My mom is French, from New Brunswick."

He frowns. "I feel bad for the native people—they were here first, all this land and water used to belong to the Mi'kmaq, but Europeans came and...the Mi'kmaq lost territory, they lost people, due to fighting over land and European diseases. I feel terrible about that...and lately, I've been feeling how important it is to feel like you belong somewhere."

Anika nods. "Me too." Her eyes gleam and Cam wonders if she's homesick for London. "Our parents moved to England from India—Kolkata," she says.

"We've been to Kolkata lots of times," Dev tells him. "Our grandparents and all our cousins live there. It's hot and crowded there," Dev says. "But fun. Our house in London was small, and it felt horrible in the pandemic. Too small. And so quiet we couldn't even hear the underground trains. No one was going anywhere. The city was dead. It's better here—bigger. Isn't it, Anika?"

Anika nods. "In normal times, we could hear the trains running in the tunnels deep under the house. But in the pandemic, they stopped. Everything stopped. India is very...colourful. I miss our family there, and friends in London."

"I'd like to go to Scotland," Cam says. "Someday. If I have money."

Anika nods. "I hope you get to go."

She turns and gazes at the ocean and the beaches and the rocks all around. "It's kinda exciting," she says, "searching for treasure—like in a book or a movie."

"There must be treasure all over the place in England," Cam says. "I saw a news report about a guy with a detector finding a Saxon gold coin. It was 1,500 years old. If I lived in England, I'd probably be searching all the time."

Anika nods. "Yes...England has tons of history. Trouble is, it feels as if everything's been done already. Do you know what I mean? Canada feels... new to us."

Cam grins. "I s'pose..."

"The ocean's so peaceful," Dev says, gazing out over the water. "I like it when it's like this. Turn the music down, will you? I want to hear the waves."

Cam turns the fiddling to mute. Peace emerges and they sit in silence, listening to the gentle roll of the water.

Dev smiles. "I love the sounds the water makes against the boat," he says. "The water says, swish, swat, gloop, thunk."

Cam grins. "Some of the noises sound kinda like sucking, don't they? That's the sound of the water under the hull."

They listen for a few moments more, then Cam

lifts a couple of red life vests from the bottom of the boat. He flings the vests at Anika and Dev. "These should fit you two. You're both small." He picks up his own yellow vest and fastens it about his chest.

The others pull on the vests, copying Cam. He checks they've fastened them tight, then turns on the engine and swings *Ashley* out into the bay.

"You sure you'll be okay with handling *Ashley* while I dive?" he asks Anika as the boat moves smoothly through the water.

"Of course," she says with a nod.

"Don't get close to the island's rocks, obviously," he says. "Stay well away. Just keep an eye out for me. If I don't come up from a dive, raise the alarm. It's easy to steer the boat: just hold the wheel steady. On wild days it can be tricky, but not today." Cam holds the wheel lightly between his hands as they travel. "Don't jerk the wheel, that's all."

"Okay," Anika says. "Sounds okay."

They approach Wreck Island, and Cam stares at the coastal rocks and the water that swirls over and around them. Fear stirs his stomach. He's never dived near such a rocky, wave-swept coast and he's never dived alone. He wonders about putting the music on again but he needs to focus and the sounds of the water remind him he must be careful, that diving is dangerous.

He cuts the engine and the boat stops in a wide circle of ripples. He gets to his feet and drops the anchor over the bow.

Dev lets out a long sigh as he gazes at the water.

"The water looks darker here," he says, and he stares down into the depths. "I don't think you should go down into the ocean here, Cam."

"I'll be careful. It's not deep. The tide's pretty low right now."

Cam pulls off his life vest and sweater. Underneath he's wearing a blue T-shirt and long blue shorts. He turns to Anika. "Okay, I need you to hold the wheel," he says.

She steps forward and takes the wheel, wrapping her hands around the soft leather circle. "I like feeling the boat in my hands," she says. "It feels like power, like it could go vroom and just soar and bounce over the waves!"

Cam grins. "No vrooming right now."

He sits and slips off his sneakers. He reaches into his bag and pulls out long yellow flippers, which he tugs onto his feet. "If you see me waving both hands above my head, that means I'm in trouble," he tells Anika. "I don't expect that to happen. I've been snorkelling many times. I'll be fine. But if you don't see me come up, raise the alarm."

Anika lifts her cell phone from her pocket and nods. "Okay."

Cam places his snorkelling mask over his face and pulls the strap around his head. Then he slips the snorkel's long, tube-like mouthpiece between his lips. As he does so, he wonders why he lied about snorkelling. Is he trying to impress Anika?

In fact, he's only been snorkelling a few times, each time with his father. They'd explored under the waves and watched the fish and seaweed dance about. He and his dad had planned to dive together often. But that never happened because the number of fish in the ocean fell again. Cam's dad had less work and less money and his parents argued more. Cam's father didn't want to go snorkelling then. His parents split and his dad moved to Frosty Cove then on to Toronto.

As Cam steps toward the rim of his boat, his memories of snorkelling with his father crowd his mind. It had felt so good to glide weightlessly through that vivid, secret world and watch the fish as they drifted and darted about. He'd felt so alive— the underwater world is so wonderful—and he'd felt a strange blend of emotions, an awed surprise combined with a familiarity, a recognition, that made him feel he should have been born a whale or a turtle.

His dad would be angry if he could see Cam now, diving alone, without a buddy. His dad always stressed safety. Safety in diving means diving with another person, so they can help each other if they get into trouble.

But Dad's gone, Cam thinks, as he climbs over the side of the boat and lowers his legs into the ocean. *I must look out for myself—and Mom.*

The cold water hits his skin, and Cam's body shrinks, recoils. *Just get on with it,* he tells himself.

He puts his face in the water and sees the island's rocky shore from below the waterline. It feels strange to see the island he knows so well from this submerged angle. The rocks seem to gleam, as if they are hiding secrets.

Cam raises his face to the surface and takes a couple of deep breaths. He fills his lungs with air then pushes his tongue over the snorkel's mouthpiece and flips downwards. Face first. He kicks his feet and dives.

Carol Moreira

22: You need to know when to fight

Cam starts exploring at one end of the island and moves slowly along. He can hold his breath for more than 60 seconds. He trained with his dad by practising underwater somersaults when he was young. Cam had been proud to reach 10 somersaults in a row within 60 seconds, no breaths. Now, he can manage a few seconds longer so that's what he does.

He explores one stretch of the rocky island, rises for air then submerges again. It isn't difficult—the tide is relatively low.

The rocks glow grey in the yellow sunlight that filters through the clean, clear water. It's strange to think how ancient these rocks are, millions of years old. Sir Stamford seems to have lived a long time ago, but 1815 is no time when compared to the age of the planet. Nonetheless, the dead sea captain has proven as hard to read as the ancient rocks beneath Cam's hands.

Cam hopes he doesn't discover a broken limb of a wreck slumped against the coast. That would be upsetting. He fears finding human bones. He wants a big, valuable treasure trove, not reminders of long-ago tragedy.

What's that?

Through the dark water, Cam sees objects glimmering on the sand below. There's half a tea cup. And, farther away, there's a collection of broken objects he can't identify. There are old things. Valuable things, maybe.

He makes himself move slowly. Divers can get caught in wreckage, caves and currents. Being trapped down here would be a nightmare.

He goes deeper, closer to the shiny objects on the sand, and his pulse accelerates. He reminds himself he doesn't believe in ghosts, but he feels almost as if he's in a graveyard. He feels he should be solemn, respectful. These objects were made and owned by people now dead.

His lungs start to ache for air. He pushes himself up to the surface of the ocean, grabs an energizing gulp of oxygen, then dives again.

Near the objects on the sand, he sees a darkness on the rock face. He pauses. It's the small, irregularly shaped mouth of an underwater cave. He stares at the cave-mouth. It looks sullen, pouty, like unhappy human lips.

As Cam watches, a cup, intact apart from its missing handle, washes from the cave-mouth and begins to drift with the current. Cam's pulse jumps. It seems his theory about the underwater cave is correct. He feels pleased, then wishes he'd thought of a cave sooner.

Instinctively, he reaches for the cup then realizes

the pressure in his lungs is becoming painful. He needs air. He kicks for the surface.

"Are you okay?" Cam hears Dev's voice echoing over the water as he emerges.

Cam gives Dev the thumb's up and breathes deep. He hauls in lungfuls of air and treads water. He looks down. The cave seems to be calling to him, promising wealth and the chance to stay here, in his own place, his own home.

He fills his lungs and kicks hard, submerging fast. He needs to get a good look at the cave. Maybe he'll venture into it, just a little bit—he doesn't want to get trapped in there.

He is almost at the cave-mouth when the water grabs him. His heart lurches as a powerful, cold wave seizes him and shoves him back and away from the cave.

Riptide!

Riptides flow from the shore out into the ocean and carry people away, exhausting them so they drown while struggling for shore. Cam knows this, and fear pulses through him, but he must stay calm.

He recalls what his father told him: *if you get caught in a rip current, don't fight.* He hears his father's voice clearly—*let the riptide carry you. After a while, it will weaken and you can swim parallel to shore to escape it. Then you can return to land.*

To practise this, Cam's dad took him to the wide and wild Salmon River when he was a kid, just eight or nine. He told Cam to first swim against the strong current, then let his body relax and be carried by it.

He and Cam got into the water and let the current take them. Cam instinctively tried to swim against the flow of water. When he fought, he found himself being swept away. But when he did as his dad said and quit fighting, the current eventually carried him toward the riverbank. Then he was able to grab a low-hanging branch and climb out.

"See?" his dad said with a big grin as he followed Cam up the bank and paused to shake the water from his dark curls. "That's how you survive, son. In this life you need to know when to fight and when to let go."

Cam had grinned at his dad as he felt his heart slow to its normal rhythm. Even with his father swimming nearby, ready to rescue him, Cam had felt powerless, had feared he might drown. The force of the water felt overwhelming.

Now, Cam tries to let his body still, to let the current take him. But it's hard, against his instincts, to go with the force of the water when he is alone and trapped beneath the surface. And he needs air. The pressure on his lungs is building. He longs to fight the riptide.

Wait. In a minute, it'll push you up.

But the weight on his lungs increases and he wants to breathe so badly he almost opens his mouth to gulp sea water. It feels as if the entire ocean is pressing on his chest. His lungs could be crushed by lack of air and the weight of water. It's like drowning in concrete. Who knew water could be so heavy?

Wait. Soon it will let you go. It feels almost as if his father's voice is inside him, speaking in his head.

And suddenly he is released. He is floating on the surface of the ocean.

Amazed, he blinks and gasps in the bright sun. In the distance, he sees the shape of his boat—so tiny, so far away—bobbing about. Anika and Dev are staring down at the spot where he entered the water.

He wants to shout and wave, to tell them, 'I'm over here,' but he is exhausted. He can't even lift his arms.

Carol Moreira

23: Don't move the wheel an inch

Dev scans the ocean. "Anika, look!" he shouts.

Anika sees Cam's head floating far away on the surface. "What's he doing out there?"

"I don't know." Dev's eyebrows furrow. "We must save him."

"But he's not waving his arms over his head," Anika says. "He said he'd wave if he was in trouble."

Just then, Cam's arms lift above his head.

"Oh no!" Dev cries.

Anika's pulse speeds up and she stares at the switches on *Ashley*'s control panel. She's nervous of the boat but reminds herself it isn't hard to control.

She remembers the anchor and runs to the side of the boat and hauls it up. The anchor feels heavy and serious in her hands as she places it in the bottom of the boat and returns to the control panel. "First, you switch on the engine..."

She turns the key and the boat throbs awake. "You steer..."

Anika feels the boat's power beneath her hands. She turns it in a wide arc and makes for the middle of the bay where Cam floats in the water.

"Are you okay, Cam?" Dev leans over the side of the boat as they approach.

Cam nods. Anika sees that Cam is too tired to talk. Weakly, he lifts his arms toward her.

"You'll have to hold the steering wheel, Dev," Anika says as she slows the boat to a crawl and steers close to Cam. "You must steer the boat absolutely straight. Don't move the wheel an inch or you'll run him over."

Dev nods and Anika carefully turns the engine to its lowest setting and lets Dev take the wheel. "Don't move the wheel even a tiny bit, Dev," she warns.

Dev nods again; his little face is set and serious.

Anika leans out of the boat and reaches down toward Cam as it comes close to him. Bracing her legs and body against the boat, she gets her arms around Cam's shoulders.

It's like the sea is sucking at them both, and she thinks it might pull her right out of the boat, but slowly she drags Cam from the water. The boat bobs in the current and Cam is heavy. Anika is glad she's in good shape.

She feels the strength in her legs and arms and rejoices—she feels strong and capable. Still, she's glad that Cam is able to use his own legs to lever himself into the boat.

Against her hands, his skin feels cold. He is trembling. She trembles too, afraid suddenly of the ocean.

"What happened?" she asks as Cam collapses, coughing and shivering in the bottom of the boat.

He shakes his head, "Tell...minute."

Anika grabs Cam's jacket from the bench and tucks it tight around him. "Keep that over you."

She drops the anchor over the side and then switches off the engine. *Ashley* bobs on the ocean, safe for now.

Anika watches Cam's face and is relieved to see his gasping breaths slow. She feels her own heartbeat calm, too, and breathes deeper.

Dev is beside her, and she whispers to him, "Did you see? I hauled him right out of the water. I think that makes me a hero, too, like him?"

Dev grins and falls laughing against the side of the boat. "Anika! You're no hero! You're just...Anika."

Anika chuckles. She feels lit up, joyful. Cam is going to be okay.

"You wait, Dev," she says. "I've got my Wonder Woman costume at home; just wait till I change into it, then you'll see what a hero I am."

She hears Cam chuckle and looks down to see him grinning up at her. "You sure seem like Wonder Woman to me right now," he says.

Carol Moreira

24: Do you want the treasure?

"What do we do now?" Anika asks. She strides about the beach and gazes at the water. *It looks so harmless from here.* "How can we get the treasure if it's so dangerous?"

"We can't," Dev says. "Forget it, Anika. Forget it, Cam."

Dev stands and plucks a pebble from his pocket, throwing it in a wide arc off Cam's deck. They watch it soar toward the water. "Darn." Dev shakes his head as the pebble sinks with just a small ripple. "How do you skim stones, Cam?"

Cam grins. "You need a flat stone—that one was too big—and you need to throw it low over the water. Here..."

He stands and walks over to Dev. "Do you have any flat stones in those pockets?"

Dev puts his hand in the left pocket of his shorts and pulls out a fistful of stones. Cam examines them as if they were emeralds. "This one looks good," he says, taking the flattest stone from the little boy's hand.

Turning toward the ocean, he throws the stone,

making it skip once, twice, three, four times before it sinks.

"That's awesome," Dev says.

Cam shrugs. "Not bad, I've done better."

"I want another turn," Dev says.

Anika frowns. "Forget the stones," she says. "What about the cave, Cam? What about the riptide?"

Cam sits down and picks up his mug of hot chocolate. He takes a long sip and looks at the ocean. The water is calm and peaceful. Some days it's hard to believe how crazy and unpredictable the ocean can be, how much chaos and struggle happen out there. One summer, his dad helped rescue whales trapped in fishing gear. It was dangerous work: the rescuers had to lean out of the boat and cut the ropes from the whales with a knife strapped to the end of a long handle.

His dad didn't talk much about those experiences, although Cam asked many questions. His dad said the whales were indescribable, that looking into the anguished eye of a trapped whale was heart-breaking and humbling.

A lobster fisherman had been killed after releasing a trapped North Atlantic right whale. He lived on Campobello Island in New Brunswick, and worked in a whale rescue operation. Over the years, he had released many whales who'd been trapped in fishing gear. But this time, after he cut away the lines around the right whale, the animal flipped, catching the bow of the boat and the man with its tail. Everyone mourned him and said he died a hero.

They were right. Cam understands why his dad didn't speak much about his experiences with whales. Words can't capture the biggest things. Words don't really say much at all.

Now, Cam turns to Anika and shrugs. "I didn't know about the riptide. I googled it. It said rip currents can appear suddenly on any beach. Big storms cause them because they churn the water up. The larger the waves, the stronger the current. It's weird. Yesterday, the water was calm. There were no big waves on that side of Wreck Island, but still there was a really strong current..."

Anika frowns. "Wow, that means you were lucky. On another day, a normal day, when the waves are bigger, the current could be worse."

Cam nods. "And rip currents can stay in one place for ages, up to a year."

He takes another sip of his drink. He feels cold, realizing how close he came to disaster. He was stupid to dive alone. He will never tell anyone he did that. "I really want to find out what's in that cave." He shakes his head, "But—"

"You don't want to drown." Dev finishes Cam's sentence for him. "You can't go back down there, Cam," he says as he sits down and reaches for another chocolate chip cookie.

There's a long silence. Dev strokes Mick, and Anika and Cam stare at the water and wonder what to do. Inside the house, the realtor is showing another group of people around. Their voices float through Cam's open bedroom window.

"Such a pretty house, lovely view of the ocean," a woman says.

"Yes," the realtor agrees, "Beautiful. Everyone values an ocean view and access. This house has both, and plenty of room for a boat."

Cam scowls. He almost wishes someone would hurry up and buy the house. He's sick of having strangers staring at his home and stuff.

"At least some treasure is washing up along the shore." Anika lowers her voice so the people upstairs won't hear. "We can keep collecting that stuff."

Cam gazes at her. "Yes, but…" He doesn't want to tell Anika about John. After the riptide, he's even less keen to get in another fight with John.

"What?" Anika demands.

Cam sighs. He and Anika will soon be in school. At school she'll learn how much John hates him. His cheeks heat when he thinks how bad he'll feel when John shoves him and calls him 'midget' in front of Anika.

"A friend of mine…John, he's hanging out along the shore, looking for stuff too. He…he's not my friend anymore. It's got ugly between us."

Anika sticks out her chin. "He sounds like a prat."

"A prat?" Cam feels his mouth twitch into a grin. Her accent sounds so sharp and judgmental. "Is that like…" He glances at Dev and lowers his voice, "a dickhead?"

She nods. "I suppose."

"I'm just trying to avoid trouble," Cam tells her.

"Why did John stop being your friend?" Dev asks.

The kid doesn't miss much.

Cam shrugs. "Our dads had a fight about fishing. There's not enough fish anymore, not enough work. Everyone competes."

"The fish were over-fished for years," Anika says. "My mum says the cod stocks fell in the 1990s and haven't recovered."

Cam shakes his head; he feels irritated to hear Anika talk about fishing as if it's a subject in school, like it's an exam and she will get 100 percent.

"The fish'll come back," he says. "Lobster and halibut are still doing well."

"Lots of species are threatened by climate change," Anika continues as if she hasn't heard him. "Carbon dioxide makes water acidic. There'll be fewer mature fish. Our mum's a marine biologist. She's got a job at the research institute in Halifax. She's planning to do some work on aquaculture."

Cam frowns. "I hate those fish farms. They look ugly on the ocean. They put all kinds of waste into the water. They mess with the wild fish."

Anika shrugs. "Fish from farms may end up being safer to eat. There's so much plastic in the water. And fishing boats have to go farther out, where the water's cooler. My mum says that makes fishing more dangerous. What about all the rogue waves? Those waves just appear suddenly and they're enormous."

"Your mom doesn't know what she's on about." Cam hears the tension in his voice, the hardness. He recalls his own dad's encounter with a rogue wave.

"The waters are cool around here. And clean. We'll be all right."

Anika's head swings again. She looks like a teacher at the front of the class—so sure she's right. "Actually, Cam, lobster stocks are up because the water's warmer, but if it warms much more, the lobsters will move north or die. And the acid in the water corrodes lobster shells."

Cam scowls and breathes deep—she's being so annoying. "Fishermen will find a way, Anika. We have to or we'll soon be a ghost town. Even the tourists will disappear when there's no one left here, when there's no restaurants and restrooms and gift shops."

"I don't know why you like fishing so much," Anika says.

Cam feels sad suddenly instead of angry. "Maybe I won't be a fisherman," he says. "I used to go out with my dad. I loved it, but maybe I won't get a place on a boat. I certainly won't have the money for my own rig. My granddad had a rig but he couldn't sell it to my dad because of the taxes. Only guys with big money or big debts have their own rigs now. It's a lot of stress. Some guys take drugs to cope."

He gazes at the water, feels a longing to be out there, surging along on the waves. "But you're your own boss out there, that's a great thing. And the ocean's always changing— it's never the same, never boring."

He turns to Anika, needing her to understand why he cares. But why would she? He can't really explain it, and she is from another world. But she nods and gazes into his eyes for a long time. She says nothing and he feels embarrassed and wonders if he's said too much, revealed too much. At least he's shut her up.

She turns back to the water. "Did John see the treasure you found?"

Cam nods. "A few things. He saw a ladle and tried to take it, but Mick scared him off." He chuckles. "Mick chewed on John's shorts."

"Good boy, Mick!" Anika reaches out and strokes the dog. Mick opens one sleepy eye and thumps his tail on the deck.

"Well then," Anika says. "We'll take Mick along with us and John will leave us alone."

Cam frowns. It's the obvious answer, but it isn't enough. Cam has loved Stony River and the beach all his life, but it does feel different now. He's resolved to ignore John but things feel...spoiled.

"You didn't speak to your dad about the fight?" Anika says.

Cam shakes his head. "No." He stares at the water. Anika's only trying to help, but she asks so many questions. She has too many opinions. Maybe it's because her parents are academics.

He smiles to himself as he recalls what his grandfather used to say about the educated government people who ran the fishery: *They've got lots of university degrees but no common sense, no idea about the real world.*

"Well, do you want the treasure, or don't you?"

Anika demands.

Cam sighs and nods. He does. "Let's go now."

He gets to his feet—might as well get on with it. And it does feel good to have Anika and Dev with him. For once, he is not alone.

25: Those white sluggy things

Mick jumps up and runs ahead, bouncing along the path to the beach. When they arrive, they find the sand covered in sand dollars.

"Wow!" Dev throws up his arms. "Where did all these new ones come from?"

"They must have been thrown up by the storm," Cam says. "The big waves churn stuff up."

Dev stares at the sand as if he can't believe his luck. Then he starts scouting around for the best sand dollars and tucking them away in his pockets. "I'll have to throw some of my stones away," he says after a minute. "My pockets are too full to fit new sand dollars in."

He frowns. "I don't want to throw my stones away."

"Collect the sand dollars later, Dev," Anika says. "Let's check the shore for treasure first."

"Don't worry, Dev," Cam says. "I'll put some of your sand dollars in my pockets." *Dev can keep the best ones*, Cam thinks. The tourists can't always have the best stuff.

They make for the shore near the river. When they

reach it, they all gasp to see a battered golden goblet, three broken plates and a slender vase lying among the slimy green seaweed.

Dev swoops on the goblet. "Amazing!" he shouts.

Anika picks up the vase. "This is so lovely." She turns it in her hands. It's covered in crusty white seaweed, but there is gold and a bit of a blue pattern shining through. She rubs the vase with her finger but can't get the crust off. "I wonder what this will fetch on eBay, Cam."

"I don't know." Cam glances down the beach to the concealing trees and back toward Wreck Island. *Maybe John is there, watching.*

Anika opens her backpack. "Let's put the treasure in here." She grins at Cam. "Don't worry. I won't steal it."

"I'll set Mick on you if you do."

"Oh, I'm sooooo scared." Anika rolls her beautiful eyes.

"I'm going to collect sand dollars now," Dev says and he strides back up the beach. After a couple of paces, he stops and stares at the sand at his feet. "Cam, come see! There's weird things."

Anika and Cam walk over and see tiny animals floating in a rock pool. "They've been swept out of the ocean and dumped in the rock pool by the big storm," Cam tells Dev as he kneels to get a better look. Cam always loves seeing the tiny creatures the waves wash up.

Dev wrinkles his nose as he peers into the rock pool. "Those white sluggy things are gross."

"But the silver fish are pretty." Anika crouches and puts her hand in the water to catch a fish, but it just swims around her fingers as if her hand isn't there. "The seaweed feels soft and fuzzy," she says.

Dev sticks his hand in. "Ew—slimy." He pulls his hand straight out.

"It's only seaweed, Dev." Anika waves her fingers around in the silky water.

"Watch out, there's a crab coming to pinch you," Dev says.

Anika sees a tiny crab making straight for her fingers and yanks her hand out.

Dev laughs. "Ha— nearly got you! Cam, should we put the animals back in the ocean?"

Cam shakes his head. "We might hurt them. They'll be okay. The high tide will eventually lift them back."

Anika stands and checks her phone. "I forgot the time. Dev, we've got to go. We'll check the rock pool later. We'll collect more treasure and more sand dollars."

"Okay." Dev jumps up and runs across the beach. "My eyes are lasers," he shouts over his shoulder. "My hungry eyes will find all the treasure and all the sand dollars."

"Hungry eyes?" Cam turns to Anika.

Anika grins. "Dev thinks he sees everything. And you know what, he does."

Carol Moreira

26: Prat

Cam feels his whole body go tense and stiff with alarm. John is standing on the rocks that line Wreck Island's seaward side. He is wearing a snorkel and flippers and staring out at the water.

Cam glances about, wishing he was somewhere else. He's only here because he wanted to see if he could spot any valuables spewing out of the under-water cave.

The way John is staring at the water alarms him. *John is going to jump in the water.*

He steps forward. "John," he shouts. "There's a rip current. Don't go in."

John turns. His face darkens. He hasn't heard Cam clamber up the island behind him. "Get lost, midget," he says.

"There's a rip current. Don't go in," Cam repeats.

He doesn't feel scared. Mick is just a few metres away, snuffling among the trees, and anyway Cam feels stronger than he did. No, it isn't himself he's worried for—it's his former best friend.

"I nearly drowned out there," Cam says.

John raises his eyebrows and smirks. His face says

Cam could drown in a bathtub.

"It's true. Some friends rescued me in my boat," Cam says. "The current swept me"—he points out into the bay—"out there. I was under the water for ages."

John glances back at the ocean. He seems to hesitate. He turns to Cam, "What friends?"

"You don't know them."

"Right." John nods as if Cam is talking about the kind of imaginary friends little kids have.

"I'm not making them up," Cam says. "You've probably seen them. Anika and her little brother Dev?"

"You mean that cute, dark girl?"

"You could describe her that way."

"Why did she come here?" John says. "We don't want new people. We've got enough problems."

Cam feels anger heat his face. "She's a good person, John. Her parents are smart—scientists. New people bring new ideas, new solutions."

But John has turned back to the ocean. "Are you crazy?" Cam yells. A band of tension grasps his head. "There's rocks, too, John. You could hit one diving from here."

John doesn't move, and time seems to pause.

Cam finds his mind filling with memories of the many good times he's spent with John—the two of them messing around in a canoe, the two of them climbing trees, shooting basketballs, laughing on the beach and Wreck Island, on their decks. If something happens to John, those will be the things Cam remembers.

He thinks of John's mom. He knows her almost as well as his own mother. What will he tell her if John drowns? What will he say?

John turns, looks up at him. "I know these shores, Cam—better than you."

"You don't know rip currents," Cam says. "I bet you've never been caught in one."

"If I get into trouble, you can save me," John says with a sneer. "Or your friends can."

Cam feels rage fill his body. "You're such a dick, John. What's wrong with you?"

He begins clambering down the rocks toward John. "Just wait," he yells. "Just wait. Do you want to drown?"

He stops on the rocks near his old friend. The two of them are close, face to face, for the first time in ages.

Cam blinks, partly with fear for John and the rip current, partly with fear *of* John. At least John is still here, still glaring at him, and not in the water.

"Why are you being such a dick about every-thing?" Cam says. He recalls rumours he heard at the restaurant that John was getting friendly with Phil McKenzie. Everyone knows Phil's dad smuggles il-legal smokes. Cam hadn't credited the rumours, but now he wonders.

"It's not my dad's fault about the fish, and it's not my fault," he tells John. "We just want to be able to stay here and make a living, like everyone else."

John shakes his head. "Maybe, but your dad...he's the dick. I told you—he took a swing at my dad over a place in Jack's boat."

Cam pauses. He still can't bear to think of his father swinging a punch at a friend. It could be true; his dad's been so...desperate.

"I bet your dad was angry, too," Cam finally says. "None of us know what to do. We just want to save our jobs and stay here. Who wants to work in a city bar? Who wants to live on an oil rig?"

John glares at Cam, then he turns and stares back at the water. Cam waits for him to jump. *Maybe it's not surprising*, Cam thinks. John was always the kid who liked to do crazy stuff. In winter, he greased his sled to make it go quicker. He rode his bike fast too and refused to wear a helmet.

Cam used to love that John was daring. John was Cam's most exciting friend. With John, Cam always felt something fun or dangerous would happen, but now Cam realizes John can take things too far.

"You know it's true, John," he says desperately. If he can keep talking, John might decide not to leap. "You feel the same as me. None of us want to go out west or to Toronto. My dad doesn't like Toronto."

Still, John says nothing, but his shoulders slump. Cam has an idea, a glimmering of understanding. "Is your dad going out west, John?"

"Maybe." It's just one word but it's enough. Cam hears the sadness in John 's voice, the fear beneath the aggression.

"We shouldn't fight," Cam says. "We've got to stand together. We have to stand up to people who blame us when things go wrong." He hears the emotion in his voice and he blinks hard. "We've *got* to, John. We're the ones who've been here, the ones who know the water. My granddad used to say fishermen are the stewards of the oceans. Maybe we've not been good stewards, but that's what we should be. It's what I want to be."

John says nothing. He keeps staring at the water. Cam feels hope slipping away—he has no words left. He watches the side of John's face and thinks this may be the last time he sees his friend. Cam blinks hard—despite everything, he can't bear to think of anything happening to John.

But finally, John turns, and a grin moves over his face, softens his hostile eyes. "That was quite a speech O'Connell. You should be a bloody politician." A small frown crinkles his brow. "Maybe we can get along again...someday."

Cam decides to ignore the 'someday'. John will always be a bit of a dick. What was that word Anika used, 'prat'? But at least John's not about to drown.

"Maybe I will become a politician one day," Cam says. "Dunno. As long as I can live near the ocean and look after fish and fishers, stay here, stay home."

Carol Moreira

27: Different shades

Anika's heart is beating a little too fast as she approaches Blueberry Island. She doesn't know why she's nervous, it just seems a strange thing to be doing, attending a blessing ceremony on an island she's never visited in a country that isn't hers.

Curiosity brings her here. And something deeper, maybe—a need to understand Nova Scotia, to try to connect rather than to just admire and criticize. A native woman will lead the ceremony, the sign in the store window said, an elder of the local Mi'kmaq.

As she'd stood in the street reading the words, Anika had felt compelled to attend. To do so, she'd needed to distract Dev and her father to get a few hours alone.

In the end, it hadn't been hard to get away. She'd told her dad and brother that she was going out to meet up with a girl of her own age. Dev had looked dubious but Anika said she'd met the girl when she'd gone to get milk and fruit at the store, and Dev couldn't argue with that.

Now Anika wishes she did have a friend to go to the ceremony with. She feels alone as she joins the group of people walking across the sandbar to the island. They are mostly a lot older than her. There are a few little kids and they are with parents.

Anika walks alone. She can feel people glancing at her with curiosity, but she pretends not to notice. She doesn't want to be talked to just because she is different and stands out.

The atmosphere feels serious as they cross the sandbar. *It's like we're going into a church or something, Anika thinks, I hope it's not going to be intense or weird.*

She glances behind her as she crosses the sandbar, back up the beach. It isn't too late to change her mind. *No*, she tells herself. *Don't be a coward—don't run.*

She follows the stream of people as they stroll up a little path between trees. They are walking across the island, Anika realizes, as she sees glittering blue ocean on either side of the path. It doesn't take long as the island is tiny, just like Wreck and Shadow Islands.

When they reach the far side, Anika sees an old woman, her grey hair covered in a bright red headscarf. The woman is sitting on a large white rock by the water. She smiles as the walkers approach, and the grin lifts her wide face and reaches her kind brown eyes. She reminds Anika of her mother's mum in India, and she relaxes, softens, a little.

"Welcome. Please sit," the elder says, spreading her hands to indicate other large rocks that seem to be arranged in a circle. "Please sit on a rock if, like me, you need support. Maybe you younger ones can sit on the ground. But please do sit in a circle."

Anika does as asked. Being young, she sits on the sandy earth, while an older man and a woman slip onto rocks on either side of her.

"Welcome," the elder says again. She has ribbons fluttering on the breast of her white blouse. The woman's eyes roam the group. "Welcome to this island, which has been an ancestral home to my people since before recorded time began."

The elder's eyes drift over the water to another nearby island. "My people used to hunt and fish these islands. Over there, on Whale Island, there are ancient graves, the remains of my Mi'kmaw ancestors." She smiles. "We are sitting on sacred earth."

Anika gazes at the woman. She can't imagine what it feels like to have such an ancient historical connection to a place. Anika misses London but her ancestors lived in India—her grandparents and most of her family are still there. *Maybe I'm not really from anywhere*, Anika thinks with a stab of self-pity. *Maybe I'm...lost.*

"To bless the island and ourselves, we light a sacred fire," the elder says. "We burn sage, tobacco, sweet grass, cedar. They will purify the rocks, the trees, the sand. They will purify us."

She leans forward and Anika notices a gentle fire is burning in a small earth-coloured container at the woman's feet. The elder reaches into a pouch that hangs from her waist and brings out a handful of something powdered and green. She scatters the mixture onto the fire and it catches, grows, licks.

Anika smells the mingled rich sweet scents. She breathes deep, remembering the spices used in the kitchens of her grandmothers in Kolkata. The Indian spices have such strong scents—they smell much fresher, more alive, than the spices her parents bought in London.

The elder struggles to her feet and picks up the container. She turns to the man sitting at her left. He stands and the elder moves forward and holds the fire before him. He reaches out, uses both hands to waft the smoke up into his face.

"We cleanse ourselves in the sacred smoke," the elder says. "We wash away our negativity."

And she moves on to the next person, who also rises and wafts the smoke over themselves.

Anika's heart beats fast in her chest. She feels embarrassed to stand and wash herself in smoke. But she is here and everyone else is doing it. She will have to do the same or be rude, foolish.

Anika gets up and meets the eyes of the elder who stands before her, smiling. Anika reaches out her hands and lifts the smoke into her face. As she does so, she feels her self-consciousness melt away. The elder smiles into her eyes, and Anika feels unexpectedly calm, peaceful.

She sits, and watches the elder move around the group. When everyone has washed themselves in the smoke, the elder puts down the fire and picks up a long wooden stick which is decorated at one end with bird feathers. Again, she turns to the man on her left.

"Cleanse your mind that you may have good thoughts," she says as she touches his head with the feathered stick.

"Cleanse your mouth that you may speak kind words," she says as she lifts the stick near his face.

Anika blinks as her eyes blur with the smoke. She sees ash on the cheek of the man. "Cleanse your body that houses your spirit," the elder says as she taps the man's shoulders. "Taho."

The elder moves again around the group, more slowly this time, repeating her blessings. Anika feels bad for the woman. She is about the same age as her own grandmothers, and she seems to be growing tired.

This time, when she gets to her feet, Anika is less nervous. She looks the elder in the eye and tries to focus on the blessings. She wonders what her London friends will think of the ceremony when she tells them. How will she describe it? She wishes she could take photos but that would be rude. She will have to describe it in words.

When the elder has completed her second tour of the circle, she sits. She closes her eyes for a moment and breathes deeply, then opens her eyes and smiles. She glances down, to the ribbons on her chest that are lifting in the breeze.

"These ribbons represent the different shades of men—red, black, yellow, white." The elder smiles and her eyes dance. "We are apt to pay too much attention to these colours, aren't we? We humans think these colours are very important."

Some people nod and chuckle, others smile ruefully.

"These differences are just...colours," the elder says.

Anika returns the elder's smile. She closes her eyes. Is it true? Are the differences between people mere colours? It doesn't feel true, but it is a soothing and encouraging idea.

She feels very peaceful. Sitting here with strangers in this beautiful place is...calming, connecting.

"It's getting hot," the elder says, and Anika opens her eyes. The elder glances at the sky. "We should leave before we burn in the sun. And before the tide turns and covers the sandbar." She smiles once more. "It is lovely to be here but I would prefer to spend the night in my own bed."

She turns again to the ocean. "See the osprey bringing fish to its young?"

Anika looks and sees a large bird swooping over the water to a tree on the adjacent island.

"Osprey are wise birds," the elder says. "They stay in one place. They pass their nest from generation to generation."

Anika feels a flicker of unease. *That's not like us*, she thinks, *not like our family. We wander.*

"I have a gift for each of you," the elder says. "I have some sacred herbs for you to take home."

The elder passes a large brown cloth bag to the man sitting beside her. He removes a small red pouch tied with yellow ribbon, then passes the bag to the next person. Each person takes a pouch from the bag.

When the bag reaches Anika, she removes a pouch, and presses the little sack of red cloth to her nose. The sweet scent of mingled herbs fills her nostrils, and she smiles. "Thank you," she tells the elder. *What a lovely gift.* She will take it home and place it with her other treasures in the altar in her bedroom.

As the participants get to their feet and walk back across the sandbar to the mainland, Anika realizes the feeling of peace has stayed with her. The other participants also seem calm and happy. There are lots of smiles. There is warmth in the air, she thinks. Community.

As she nears her home, she sees a young fawn with its mother. The pair are feasting on the grass at the front of her house. Anika's heart beats fast, her mouth smiles. It must be the same fawn. It *must* be. She has been keeping an eye out and she hasn't seen any other fawn so young, still covered with the white spots of the newborn.

She stands, admiring the feasting animals. Then, not wanting to disturb them, she takes the back door inside, and leans for a moment against the door frame.

She can't stop smiling. Warm relief fills her. She hadn't realized how worried she'd been about the little fawn and its mother.

Her hand tightens around the red pouch in her hand. *It will get easier here*, she thinks.

It already is. Dad came back from Dalhousie more cheerful than when he left. "I think it'll be okay," he told Anika. "I like my colleagues, lovely campus."

And her mother seems content. Anika can tell her mum is happy in her new job because she is calm, often preoccupied. Anika can almost hear her mum's brain humming inside her head, like a quietly efficient machine.

"Busy at work, Mum?" she had asked the previous evening when her mother was chopping onions, a look of intense preoccupation on her face.

"Yes, dear," her mother said, glancing up. "It's interesting. There's a lot of challenges here caused by over-fishing and habitat destruction, and the water is warming faster than elsewhere. We're looking at improving data collection—we need to know exactly what's going on in the ocean."

Her mum paused; the knife stilled in her hand. "We haven't been doing much together as a family, have we? How about we all go into Halifax on Saturday? It's lovely along the waterfront, lots of maritime history. We could stroll about, get some ice cream."

Anika had grinned, happy to think of the four of them in Halifax together—maybe she needn't have worried about her parents' marriage. "Good idea. I can't believe we've only been into Halifax once," she said.

"I'm sorry, love." Her mum's brow had crinkled, and Anika thought how much she loved her mother's face—her wide, intelligent eyes, her generous mouth. "Your dad and I have been so focused on getting unpacked, settled, before the school year." Then she smiled. "Let's have some fun together?"

Anika nodded. "Shall I peel the carrots?"

"That would be great."

As Anika fetched the carrots, she had thought that things were definitely looking up.

And if Cam wants to go out with me, I'm going to, she thinks now as she moves away from the door and toward the kitchen and the sound of her brother and father talking. Mum and Dad, all the family, will just have to get used to it.

Carol Moreira

28: There's no going back

The following morning, Cam feels happier, lighter than he has in months. He can't believe it but John finally apologized, and Cam's father is coming to visit the very next day.

Cam listens to Ashley MacIsaac's fiddling as he gets ready to meet Anika and feels the upbeat tempo reflect his own mood. He smiles to himself as he pulls on his favourite blue T-shirt. He can't wait to see Anika.

He meets her at her house, then they walk to Stony River. They sit on the red-brown surface of a rock adjacent to the water and Mick throws himself onto the grass next to Cam and rests his snout on his paw.

Cam stares down into the river. It would be cool to see the rainbow trout today, with his dad coming and Anika sitting here beside him.

It would feel right.

"So, what do you fish for?" Anika asks.

"Right now, I'm looking for a special rainbow trout," Cam says. "My dad saw him swimming upstream here. He's huge and colourful. I wanted to catch him."

Anika leans forward and peers into the water.

"We have to keep dead quiet to see him," Cam says. "I doubt you can do that."

"Hey!" Anika sits up and shoves Cam, nearly pushing him off the rock. "I *can* keep quiet. It's Dev who can't. I'm glad he's found some friends his age."

Cam looks over at the shore of Wreck Island. "I'm going to tell the police about the cave and the treasure, Anika."

"What?" Her eyes are wide, incredulous.

"It's just causing trouble. People are going to get into danger, maybe even drown, when they realize it's down there. And it's not mine, anyway. It belongs in a museum—the Maritime Museum in Halifax, probably, along with the belongings of the people who died on the *Titanic*."

"But...you need the money," Anika says. "If you tell the authorities, you won't get to keep any of the stuff you found."

Cam grins. "Well, I've already sold lots of it...."

Anika sighs. "It's kinda awesome, everything lying down there, undiscovered, for so long. It's mysterious, creepy..."

Cam nods. The age of it all makes tingles run up his spine. It feels sad, too, somehow, because all the people of that time are dead and forgotten.

"But I still think you should keep some of it," Anika insists. "You found it and you need it."

Cam shrugs again. His shoulders feel loose, free. They've felt heavy for months, he realizes—rigid, like rock. "I had an idea," he says, "a way to make legit money. I thought I could give tours of Wreck Island, take tourists out on *Ashley* and tell them about Sir Stamford and the privateers. Maybe I'll tell them about my granddad's obsession with the treasure and how that got passed down to my dad, how I never believed in the treasure but finally discovered it. Do you think people would be interested?"

Anika nods. "Yes! You'll be famous when the story breaks. You could dress up as a privateer." She smiles. "You'd look good with a bandana 'round your hair."

She puts her head on one side, studies him. "Maybe a patch over one eye."

He grins. "Yeah, it could be fun—better than working in the restaurant, better than harvesting and collecting stuff for the tourists."

Anika nods, but she sighs again and her eyes cloud. "School starts soon. I'm nervous about starting a new school in a new country. I mean I want to get back to school—I want to be a marine biologist, like my mum. And I didn't like studying online during the pandemic. I want—I need—to be with people. But...I'm...nervous."

Cam is surprised. He can't imagine Anika being nervous about anything. "It'll be okay," he says. "You'll be fine."

"Cam, I'm scared some people might be...racist."

Cam's heart jumps at the thought of people being mean to Anika. "Really? Well...you tell me, tell the staff." He stares into her eyes. "Promise me you will,

Anika. Don't put up with any crap from anyone."

She nods. He sees relief in her eyes. "I promise," she says.

"Were people racist in London?" he asks.

"Sometimes. But mostly it was good because London is so diverse. I feel weird here because…I'm the only one. Almost everyone here is white. People look at me. Their eyes make me feel like I'm an alien. Your friend John told me to go home, he said people don't want people like me here. After that, when I saw him, I hid. Now I'm scared of seeing him at school, scared other kids might be like him."

"When did this happen?"

"A while ago."

"Why didn't you tell me?"

Anika shrugs. "I didn't know what to do…"

Cam shakes his head. "Well, he's going to apologize to you, like he apologized to me. If he doesn't, I'll tell everyone at school he's a racist. John likes—he really needs—to be popular. I'm sorry you've had bad experiences here, Anika. But, like I said, don't put up with it."

Cam sighs, not knowing what else to say. All he can do is try to help.

He thinks about John's apology to him. He'd felt stunned and so relieved that John hadn't dived off the island, that they were talking again, he'd told John, 'It's okay, forget it.' In fact, a little nub of resentment lingers in Cam's heart. He isn't sure the two of them can ever be close again like they were. Now, this news of Anika's makes it seem unlikely.

"You want a shortbread?" He reaches into his pocket and brings out a brown bag full of smooth yellow cookies. "My mom can't stop baking since... everything." He pats his belly. "I better watch it, or I'll never make the football team."

Anika takes one. "Your mum bakes the best stuff." Surprisingly, she's finding out that some Canadian baking is really good.

"Look..." She points with her cookie. "Is that the special fish?"

Cam looks down and sees a long, dark body moving upriver toward them. The big fish is swimming by himself with several smaller fish following behind.

"Yes!" Cam feels his mouth lift in a grin. It's a shock, a thrill, to finally see the special trout.

But another part of Cam isn't surprised. He feels almost as if he and the fish had arranged to meet that day.

The trout is big and powerful, although he isn't all the rainbow colours his dad talked of. There are a few bright splashes of yellow and blue-green, but it seems his dad exaggerated the colours.

Well, his dad often exaggerates. Yesterday, Cam's mom said again that his dad has too much imagination. Maybe she's right. Cam doesn't care. Life would be dull without imagination, and he likes his dad the way he is—mostly.

They watch the fish as he moves around, exploring the little rocks and floating plants in the water. Then he flicks away and swims upriver.

Cam watches him go. He doesn't wish he had his fishing rod with him. He wouldn't have wanted to catch such an amazing fish. He could not have made himself snap that trout's neck. He couldn't have gutted him and left his entrails for the gulls. Even catching and releasing him would have felt wrong. Cam wants that fish to remain free.

"He *is* beautiful." Anika watches the fish until he's gone. "I wish he'd stayed longer."

Cam nods. "Me too. He's a sea-running trout that likes to explore along the coastline. He's adventurous, not like brook trout that live their whole lives in safe water."

They sit in comfortable silence. Then Cam says, "My father's coming tomorrow. He's going back to school to train as a welder. Dad misses the ocean. He wants to work at the Halifax Shipyard. He doesn't like Toronto, and the pandemic hit bars and restaurants so hard they still haven't come back. But it means I can keep *Ashley*."

Anika grins. "That's awesome!"

Cam pauses. There's something else to tell her, something painful he hopes he can relate without choking up. "My dad's got a girlfriend. They're going to have a baby. Mom told me. She's upset, obviously."

He stops, sadness squeezing his throat. His mom had cried as she related the news. "It's final now, Cam," she'd said. "There's no going back."

Cam had gathered his mother in his arms. He knew what she meant. Another family meant his dad was gone for good, had other responsibilities. Cam knew his dad would now have even less time for him.

But he'd stood tall with his arms around his mother, and he'd felt his own strength. He might have inherited his mother's small stature, but he was strong.

I'll look out for Mom, he thought. *I have to, and I want to.* It occurred to him that maybe he was nearly there, maybe he was already nearly the man he was going to be.

"I'm sorry about your dad, Cam." Anika's eyes are so warm and kind Cam fears she'll make him cry.

"We had to sell our house," he tells her. "But Mom found one nearby so we don't have to move far. We're moving to Bedford Lane."

As he speaks, he thinks of the quiet little street that leads from his home to the village store. He has walked it his whole life. It feels so familiar, it won't be so bad to live there.

"Mom never wanted us to leave here," he says, and he recalls how his mom smiled when she told him about the new house.

"I tried to tell you before that I was looking at a house on Bedford Lane, Cam. Not Bedford in Halifax. But you cut me off, you wouldn't listen. I decided to let you wait and see..." Her grin grew wider. "You should have known that I'd do the best I could, Cam, for both of us. I knew you didn't want to move to the city."

"I'm sorry, Mom," Cam had said. *I've been a dick, myself,* he'd thought. *Treating Mom like she's an idiot.*

"Bedford Lane will be okay," he tells Anika now. "But I don't think I'll like walking past our old house. That'll make me feel bad."

"Walk down a different street then," Anika says. "Walk on the beach. I'm so happy you're staying in the village."

"Me too. I'm so relieved we're not moving to Halifax," Cam said. "That's what so many of our people do—move for a job, an opportunity. It sounds weird, but I'm scared I'd lose myself in a city—not know who I am."

Anika nods. "It is hard, moving somewhere new. Everything's strange and you don't know anyone. You can feel like...someone else...someone emptier, stupider, than you were before."

"Do you still miss London?" Cam says.

She nods and dips her head. "I do..." She looks up. "But living here is a new experience. I feel in that way that life has got...bigger."

"Good." Cam looks over at Wreck Island and realizes that lately he's been feeling like an island himself—a lonely island surrounded by cold, threatening water. He's felt that way because of John and his dad, maybe. Now, he feels his shoulders loosen again. He breathes deep. He feels like he's been holding his breath for years.

He turns to Anika. "Do you think you'll like it here —I mean, really feel at home—after a while?" It seems like a very important question.

She shrugs. "I dunno. I miss London, like I said. But I always miss my family in Kolkata too, especially when we first leave them, so...I am looking forward to winter in Canada. London doesn't get very cold."

Cam nods. "Winter's long here, but there's skiing, snowboarding, skating...Hockey, too—if you're fast enough, and tough enough."

Anika smiles. "I don't know how tough I am, but I think this place will teach me."

"We can go paddling in my canoe," Cam says. "We can paddle on the ocean and there's a big lake near here. That's if Your Ladyship doesn't mind me showing you a lake in my own country that I've known about my whole life?"

Anika's cheeks turn rosy. "I'm sorry I was like that —rude, ungrateful. I'd love to go in your canoe."

Her brown eyes smile at him, so bright they seem to glow. Cam feels his heart lift like a relaxed summer wave. Something in Anika's eyes makes him brave enough to reach his hand toward hers.

She shifts toward him. Their fingertips touch, and Cam feels both the warmth and softness of her skin and the cool, rough rock beneath his palm.

He slips his fingers closer and their hands come together. Her fingers curl through his.

"I'm glad I met you, Cam," Anika says.

"Me too. I'm glad you came here," Cam replies.

He looks down at their two hands linked on the rock, and smiles to see their entwined fingers blending brown, white, brown, white.

END

Carol Moreira

Acknowledgements

As so many have said, writing often feels lonely, which makes all social opportunities as important as sunny days in winter. While researching *Riptides*, I got to spend time with some fun and kind-hearted people: Leena Roy Chowdhury and Jennifer Lee shared their experiences of life as members of Nova Scotia's BIPOC community, and Sandy Stoddard told stories of his many years spent fishing Nova Scotia's South Shore—and gifted me the best and freshest halibut and tuna I've ever tasted. Mi'kmaw historian and linguist Bernie Francis generously shared his time and expertise with me, as did Gaelic specialist Lewis MacKinnon

I'd also like to thank Gaelic expert Lewis MacKinnon for his help.

The story mentions a brave whale rescuer. This passage draws on the real-life story of Joe Howlett, who died a hero while rescuing a right whale in 2017.

I owe big thanks to the members of my writers' group who helped me hone this story: Susan Church, Alison DeLory, Melanie Furlong, Jill Hamilton, Mary Lou Petersen, and Cheri Wilson, whose friendship meant so much, especially during the grim months of lockdown.

Thanks to my husband, Peter Moreira, for introducing me to his beautiful home province, and to our children, Cat and Scott, for all the fun and inspiration.

It feels so good when a book finds the right home, and I have loved working with Andrew Wetmore, the insightful, disciplined, and humorous editor at Moose House.

And to some earlier editors who helped me along the way: Faye Smailes at Lorimer and Kat Kruger and Colleen McKie at Fierce Ink Press, thank you.

About the author

Born in Britain and raised in the U.K. and Hong Kong, Carol Moreira is an award-winning journalist who has worked around the world. A wanderer by training and inclination, she is currently based in beautiful Nova Scotia where she relishes the great outdoors.

Carol is the author of two other young-adult novels:

- *Charged (James Lorimer 2008)*
- *Membrane (Fierce Ink Press 2013)*

and is a contributor to the immigration anthology *Coming Here, Being Here* (Guernica Editions 2016).

She is a partner in entrevestor.com, an innovation news site, and is excited to be co-launching an oceans-themed publication.

* 9 7 8 1 9 9 0 1 8 7 2 0 9 *